A SUMMER AT THOUSAND ISLAND HOUSE

ROMANCE IN THE GILDED AGE
BOOK FOUR

SUSAN G MATHIS

WILD HEART BOOKS

*To the Thousand Islands River Rats, my faithful readers
who love the river as much as I do. Thanks for your support
in reading my stories, sharing them with others, and leaving
reviews. You bless me.*

*To my wonderful Beta Team, Judy, Laurie, Donna, Barb,
Melinda, and Davalynn who inspires me with your
kindness, faithfulness, and wisdom. You are dear friends,
gifts, and a precious team.*

"Susan G Mathis gives us a sweet story set during the summer of 1885 in the Thousand Islands area of New York. *A Summer at Thousand Island House* takes us on a journey with characters willing to change their attitudes and maintain enduring faith, and many historical details that will keep readers turning the pages."

— JANET GRUNST, AUTHOR OF *A HEART SET FREE*, *A HEART FOR FREEDOM*, AND *SETTING TWO HEARTS FREE*

"Once again, Mathis has captured the essence of the Gilded Age in this lovely romance. Her extensive research adds layers of realism to the setting and characters. That you-are-there feeling follows the reader to the very last page."

— CINDY ERVIN HUFF, AWARD-WINNING HISTORICAL AND CONTEMPORARY ROMANCE AUTHOR

"Award winning author, Susan G Mathis, has penned another heartfelt story. Of all she has written, this one is my favorite. *A Summer at Thousand Island House* is a story of compassion, friendship and love, but also of forgiveness. Set in 1885 in the Thousand Islands, Addison Bell and her dilemmas ring true. Through her courage and perseverance, she deals with situations many of us face today. Thank you, Susan Mathis, for this uplifting story."

— CAROL GUTHRIE HEILMAN,
AUTHOR OF *THE AGNES HOPPER SERIES*

"Susan G Mathis has written another story full of history, love, and faith. She weaves a tale of longing, intrigue, and mystery around real-life people and events. A must-read for any fan of well-written fiction."

— DONNA SCHLACHTER, HISTORICAL FICTION AUTHOR

"Author Susan G Mathis has crafted another heartwarming story with characters I loved from the first page. Get ready to laugh, cry, and sigh as you experience a unique perspective of the Gilded Age by those who serve the affluent and influential. An added bonus is the opportunity to delve into the rich history of the Thousand Islands."

— LINDA SHENTON MATCHETT, BEST-SELLING AUTHOR *SPIES & SWEETHEARTS*

"This delightful heroine has more challenge than most young women could handle, yet once again, Susan G Mathis keeps us reading and believing in Addison Bell during her harrowing stay at the Thousand Island House on Staple's Island. Don't miss this charming summer novella."

— DAVALYNN SPENCER, AWARD-WINNING AUTHOR OF INSPIRATIONAL WESTERN ROMANCE

CHAPTER 1

THOUSAND ISLAND HOUSE
ALEXANDRIA BAY, NY
SUMMER, 1885

*A*ddison Bell breathed a quick prayer as she grasped the door handle of the Thousand Island House's recreation pavilion. "Please, Lord, may this summer change my life."

She froze, a tiny tremble of her jaw betraying her resolve to be strong. What would the future hold for her at such an opulent place? Such a foreign establishment? A three-story building dedicated to nothing but recreation?

For her, a simple farm girl and one-room schoolhouse teacher from Watertown Center, this seemed unconventional—eccentric, even. Yet now, here she was, thirty miles away, at the most celebrated hotel in

Alexandria Bay, perhaps in all the Thousand Islands—late for work on her first day.

Before she had the chance to pull herself from her ponderings and enter the pavilion, someone pushed open the door she still held, sending her flying onto her backside, skirts flapping in the breeze. Her arms and legs flailed like an octopus out of water. Her carpetbag went flying too. Right into the path of a stalwart gentleman. Her gaze traveled from his toes to his nose. A naval officer, of all people.

The man tripped over her bag but somehow kept his balance. Then he turned to her with a furrowed brow as he reached for her hand, concern marring his handsome face. "Are you all right, miss?"

"Yes, thank you, sir. I'm sorry I tripped you up." A nervous giggle slipped out as she accepted his hand, her cheeks burning at the thought of her buffoonery.

The officer tugged her to her feet, and she furiously smoothed her skirts. Her well-worn straw hat flopped to one side, dangling precariously over one eye. She righted it as best she could, ignoring the pins poking into her scalp. She must look affright.

"I am the one who must apologize for opening the door and sending you aloft." He paused for a moment and tipped his hat. "Lieutenant Maxwell Worthington of the US Navy." He clicked his heels before snapping a quick nod her way. "At your service, miss."

Addi curtsied low and sucked in a steadying breath. Then she pasted on a smile. "Pleased to meet you, Lieutenant, but I must be on my way. I'm late as it is."

"Hurry then, and farewell for now." Lieutenant Worthington picked up her bag and handed it to her.

"Thank you, sir. Good day to you."

Addi regathered her nerve and turned to enter the pavilion. A man stood before her, his title of manager boldly proclaimed on his name tag.

He snapped a concerned glance at the retreating lieutenant and then at her. "Servants should enter at the back, miss. I'll excuse the mishap this once. Aye, both mishaps."

Addi blinked. A hint of Irish floated on the man's words, making them sound like a melody to a faraway tune, even as he scolded her. In public.

"Mr....Mr. Donovan?"

Her words squeaked out as if she were a tiny child. She swallowed her angst, straightening her shoulders to regain some semblance of professionalism.

The man nodded, an almost imperceptible smirk appearing, then fading fast. "Aye, one and the same. You're late. Let's get you settled."

Addi's nerves got the better of her, and her tongue took flight. "I'm sorry I'm tardy, sir. The horse threw a shoe on the way here, and the wagon went into the ditch, and Mr. Stevens didn't know what to do, but then a farmer helped us out, but—"

Mr. Donovan held up his hand to stop her chattering but cast her a kind smile. He took the carpetbag from her and motioned for her to enter the pavilion. "It's all right, miss. This is your day to settle in and prepare for the rest of the summer. You've no children waiting."

"Thank goodness." Addi sighed loudly, adjusting her teetering hat.

Once inside, Mr. Donovan paused in the foyer and tipped his head, assessing her from her still-teetering hat to her scuffed boots. "Aye, this is the Thousand Island House recreation pavilion, where you will spend the next several months caring for our patrons' children. I must say, your recommendation was quite glowing, especially from my crotchety old friend, Alvin Sanderson. But I didn't expect someone so young to be so accomplished, and from Watertown Center?"

"I'm twenty-four, sir. I've taught up to eighteen children concurrently for the past five years. All ages. All temperaments. And I have to tell you that some of those students, especially the older ones, gave me great consternation. But I overcame their podsnappery with determination and grit." Addi stood as tall as her small frame would rise and lifted her chin.

Mr. Donovan chuckled, wiping the mirth away with the sweep of his hand. "Your enthusiasm is commendable, miss, but quite unnecessary. The former nursery teacher in your position, Mrs. Randolph, barely got off her perch 'cept when it was a matter of life and death. Nevertheless, the parents and children appreciated her grandmotherly ways."

Addi harrumphed, and a small snicker escaped her lips. "I, sir, am not a grandmother, and I believe children are to be given all the fullness of experiences available. Music. Dance. Sports. Nature. Games. Play. And a good dose of God."

"Blathers! You misunderstand. We didn't hire you to teach school. You'll be caring for four-to-seven-year-olds. Mere babes out of diapers." Mr. Donovan sucked in a breath.

"Oh, I don't plan to drill them in the three R's." Addi shook her head. "I simply want to expose them to a wealth of experiences while they're under my care."

Brow knotted, he chewed on his full bottom lip as he studied her—and she him. A generous dollop of Morgan's pomade had to be keeping his curly dark hair in place, else his abundant locks would cover his strong forehead. A full head taller than herself, the man possessed a square chin and high cheekbones that reminded her of royalty, yet his demeanor cast a welcoming, friendly air, even when he frowned.

She stood her ground but turned her attention to the pavilion signs just beyond them—Game Room, Billiard Room, Bowling Alley, Children's Nursery, Men's and Women's Bathing Room, Swimming Pool, and Dancing Pavilion. The choices made her head swim. How could one choose from such lavish entertainments?

Mr. Donovan must have seen her dismay, for he began a tour without addressing her prior comment.

"This recreation facility is exclusively for our hotel patrons, though some esteemed visitors not staying at the hotel still come here now and then. As you can see, we have the most modern facilities for entertaining those on summer holiday. Upstairs are various game rooms, mostly for men, which you do not need to see. There are also a grill and garden roof where we host afternoon teas. And more." He patted the nearby desk then pointed beyond it to a tiny room. "This is the reception desk, and that's my office, should you ever need to find me, though I'm often about serving our clients or solving problems." He waved a hand, signaling the end of the brief tour. "This way to the children's nursery, miss."

Mr. Donovan led her down a long hallway. Near the end, he opened the door to a large classroom. "I must admit that your high-minded notions on childcare surprise me. The hotel provides abundant means of children entertaining themselves. Tin toys. Puzzles. Books. And this large room with an ensuite water closet. As far as your duties, you are required only to keep the children safe and quiet."

"Dear me." Addi moaned, curling her hand beneath her chin. "I don't intend to be a jail warden or a prison guard. And I do not adhere to the motto, 'children are to be seen and not heard.' I believe youngsters are like beautiful flowers that are to be nurtured and watered and allowed to blossom and grow into the creatures of beauty God intended them to be. I cannot abide stifling their innate curiosity to learn and grow. I must reinforce it."

Mr. Donovan took a step back, slapping his chest in mock shock. "Blathers! I've hired a radical! Still, you know children better than I, so I will concede to your plans."

"Please, sir. I am not a radical, nor do I mean to impute your idea of childcare, merely to enhance the summer experiences for these little ones." Addi curtsied, humbling herself before her employer.

He chuckled and set her bag on a nearby table. "I understand, but if you deem it necessary to employ your unique ideas, you must get permission from each of the parents to undertake such modern methods. I fear they will view you as merely a babysitter, not a teacher extraordinaire."

"I will, sir. Thank you, sir." Addi clapped her hands, joyful that she'd won the first battle.

She'd won, but surely, from the pluck she'd observed in this Irish manager, there'd be more skirmishes in the days to come.

* * *

*L*iam Donovan shook his head at the strange and lovely lass he'd hired and left in the nursery. Aye, her tongue took to chattering faster than a house-wren's song, but her excitement for teaching children was unmistakable and quite refreshing. Old Mr. Sanderson hadn't warned him of that. Nor of how beautiful she was, with her rich chocolate-brown hair, big, bright eyes warm as melted chocolate, and captivating smile. Blathers! That smile nearly made him go weak at the knees. Then, when she prattled on about her modern methods, it took everything in him not to fawn over her. Yet, as manager of the hotel's recreation pavilion, he had to keep his wits about him.

"Get a hold of yourself, Liam!"

He stopped cold in his tracks upon hearing his own voice.

"Did you say something, sir?" Melvin Olson stared at him with veiled amusement.

A year ago, the recreation leader for their older children and former baseball star had shattered his arm, forever ending his promising career in the sport. Now, he faithfully occupied the eight-to-fourteen-year-old children while their parents enjoyed a life of leisure.

Liam shrugged, raising his palms to the ceiling, then quickly shoving them into his pockets. "Nothing, Mel. Have you any troublemakers in your group of late?"

Melvin popped his gum. "None I can't control. Five silly girls who only want to gossip and talk about boys, and six rambunctious boys who are happy to try to outwit or outrun one another. Easy as batting five hundred."

The lad always referred to baseball, but he was good with kids, and that was what mattered. "Have you enough to keep them busy?"

Snap. "Always. The House provides plenty. Thanks for scheduling them for bowling and swimming once a week. Those'll be the highlight of their time here, without a doubt." Melvin smacked his gum as if he were punctuating his sentence. "Did the nursery teacher arrive?"

"Yes. She's in her room getting settled. I'll introduce her later."

"Fair enough. Better get back to those rascals. Thanks, sir."

Melvin took his leave with another annoying pop, snap, and crack of his gum. The lad was never without his Adams New York chewing gum. Worse than a smoker.

The habit irritated Liam to distraction. Not only was it uncouth and distracting, but it was also a bad habit to model to children. Moreover, a Thousand Island House employee needed to maintain the utmost decorum. Yes, he'd have to talk to him about it—sooner rather than later. Still, habits die hard, and he couldn't afford to offend Melvin and be without a worker right now.

As Liam returned to his desk, Miss Bell's pretty face swept back into his thoughts. Was she as bubbly and vivacious as she appeared, or was it just nerves? His Tina had been like that at first, too, but she gradually withdrew until she'd broken his heart with a rather cold rejection of his marriage proposal. Then, she'd agreed to marry him after all but only days later, left him for his best friend. Aye, well...

After addressing several management situations around the pavilion, Liam decided to check on his newest employee and get her settled in the women's dormitory. He knocked on the classroom door and entered, finding the kitchen maid, Gert, delivering a tray.

"I was told you had six children, plus yourself. Now look at the food that will go to waste." Gert's tone was icy. Harsh, even.

Liam cleared his throat to announce his arrival. "My oversight, miss. I should've sent word the children wouldn't be present today. That wasn't Miss Bell's responsibility. She just arrived an hour ago."

Gert's pudgy face turned red as a ripe tomato, and her tone became syrupy sweet. As it always did when she spoke to him and batted the lashes of her bulgy eyes. It made his stomach clench every time. "Oh, Mr. Donovan. I didn't hear you enter. It's all right. We can add the jam sandwiches to our staff luncheon." She set a wrapped sandwich on the table and glared at Miss Bell. "I'd better get back to the kitchen and help prepare the noon meal. You be certain to let me know in time from here on out."

Miss Bell nodded, a sweet smile begging pardon. Why did Gert have to be so rude?

He smiled as the kitchen maid waddled out the door, smelling of bacon grease and raw chicken. When the door clicked shut, he shrugged. "Sorry about the misunderstanding with the maid. As you've heard, lunch will be delivered to you every day at noon with a snack you can set aside for the afternoon. How do you find your classroom? Do you need anything?"

Miss Bell grinned widely. "This room is well-equipped with the newest books and toys. Thank you. But...I wondered if I might procure a terrarium."

"A what?"

The lovely lass giggled, sounding like melodic wind chimes. "A terrarium. A large glass bowl I can use to arrange plants and moss and bugs and worms and maybe even a frog or two for scientific observation and for the children's enjoyment. It's the latest thing for helping children learn about God's creation."

Liam chuckled at the unconventional request. "You're a rather bricky woman, Miss Bell."

Her brows furrowed, her doe eyes sparking confusion. "Bricky?"

Liam clicked his tongue. "Tenacious. Strong. Like a brick wall. It's meant to be a compliment. Few women would undertake a bug-infested, moss-soaked, frog-hopping science experiment."

Miss Bell waved a hand, her eyes dancing with amusement. "I'm a farmer's daughter. None of that shatters my feminine world."

"Very well, miss. I shall see what I can procure. For now, I'll escort you to the women's dormitory. Then you can familiarize yourself with the hotel and grounds and be ready for the morn." He handed her the sandwich Gert left behind. "Your lunch."

"Thank you, sir. I'd like to be well accustomed to my surroundings before the children come." Miss Bell accepted the sandwich and curtsied.

Liam picked up her carpetbag and led her outside through the back entrance. "Staff uses this door only. You will care for six children—and sometimes more—for most of the summer. You will lead the children through this entrance as well. You may use this back lawn for play as long as adult patrons are not present. But keep the noise to a minimum, please. And unless there's a special event where children are welcome, you shall not take them to the front of the pavilion and never around or into the hotel itself."

They crossed the small footbridge connecting the pavilion's island to the mainland where the hotel stood.

"Can the children swim? Bowl? Play badminton?"

Liam stopped halfway to the dormitory. "Certainly not, miss. They're babes. They must be older to participate in such activities."

Miss Bell bit her bottom lip but said nothing. Her eyes told a stormy tale of disagreement churning inside. But he'd not open that discussion just now.

Entering the two-story house that was used as the women's dormitory, Liam stopped at the door as the housekeeper joined them. "Good day to you, Mrs. Erving. This is Miss Addison Bell, the nursery worker we've been waiting for."

Mrs. Erving nodded, wiping her wrinkled hands on her apron. Then she swiped her brow with her forearm. "Very good. You'll be bunking with Gert, upstairs, first door on the right." At that, a small groan escaped from Miss Bell, though the housekeeper continued without seeming to notice. "There are two uniforms on the bed, but I daresay they may be too big. Girl, you're skinny as a toothpick! I'll have to find smaller ones."

"Yes, ma'am." Miss Bell curtsied.

Liam sighed. Poor Miss Bell, having to room with prickly Gert. Perhaps he should request a change? No, this was the housekeeper's domain, not his.

Mrs. Erving cast him a scowl and pursed her lips before speaking again. "A few rules. First, no fraternizing with men, either staff or especially not patrons. Either infraction will yield immediate dismissal." Their new nursery worker counted on her fingers as Mrs. Erving provided her list. "Second, keep your room clean and tidy at all times. Third, only women staff are allowed beyond this door." She thrust a fat hand toward the door behind them. "Fourth, no unnecessary noise. Fifth, lights out and all quiet at nine p.m. No exceptions."

Miss Bell closed her fist and clasped her hands together, her mouth pulling tight. She bobbed a curtsy. "Yes, ma'am."

Liam set down her bag and snapped a nod her way. "All right, then, Miss Bell. Get settled and acclimate to your new home. Your shift begins at eight a.m. sharp."

Miss Bell dipped a low curtsy and rewarded him

with a bright smile. "Thank you, Mr. Donovan, for this opportunity to serve."

He returned a smile. "Until tomorrow."

Why did he feel he'd be counting the hours until then?

CHAPTER 2

After Mr. Donovan departed, Addi started for the stairs, but Mrs. Erving shook her head, pointing to the sandwich in her hand. "Go and eat at the table, miss. No food upstairs. We don't need no mice or other varmints joining us."

She wasn't really hungry, but she followed the woman into the large kitchen and sat at a long table, unwrapping the sandwich and taking a bite.

Mrs. Erving handed her a plate and poured a glass of milk, placing it before her. "You need fattening up, girl. Meals are rather hodge-podge around here as work hours vary, but I am in the kitchen from five a.m. to eight p.m. If you miss those hours, you'll have to fend for yourself."

"Yes, ma'am. Thank you." She nodded, taking a sip of cold, fresh milk.

"You can call me Mrs. Erving. I also do light housekeeping, but mainly I cook. And keep you girls in line." The housekeeper cast her a warning glare as she slipped several slices of carrots and cucumbers onto her plate. Then she handed her another plate with a large piece of iced carrot cake on it. "Remember the rules, and we'll get along just fine."

Goodness! Could Mrs. Erving be as harsh as Mrs. Baumgardner? She'd boarded with the grouchy old woman after her papa died of apoplexy last year, and it had been miserable. Would history be repeating itself?

After she finished her meal and thanked the woman, she carried her carpetbag upstairs and glanced around the tiny room that was to be her new home. Two steel-framed single beds with a small table in between. A washstand and pitcher, and a four-drawer dresser. Two gray uniforms lay neatly folded on the bed. She unfolded one and held it up to her. Sure enough, made for a much larger woman. Like her roommate, Gert.

Would she find a friend in the kitchen maid? Doubtful. Would she find any in such a place? Hopefully. Watertown Center had provided relatively few, especially once her school chums married and moved away. A pang of loneliness twisted her insides. With Papa gone, she was all alone in the world. No aunts, uncles, cousins. No one.

She washed her face, refashioned her hair, and repinned her hat. Pinching her cheeks and shaking herself from her sadness, she left her bag on the bed and fled the house, determined to acquaint herself with the palatial grounds on the St. Lawrence River shoreline.

She walked along a beautiful pathway elegantly surrounded by vibrant, colorful flower beds, lichen-covered stone walls, massive shade trees, and lush green lawns. She stopped to watch butterflies and humming-birds flit from flower to flower, dancing in the sunshine. Pinks, yellows, oranges, and purples offered a heart-warming feast for the eyes. Scents of lavender, rose, and lily played with her nose until they tickled it into a sneeze.

"Ah-choo!"

She glanced around. Thankfully, no one stood near enough to hear, so she returned to enjoying the sights, sounds, and smells in this veritable fairyland. She'd bring the children here to teach them about flowers and pollination.

Pulling herself from the beauty of the garden, Addi smiled at the sign posted near an unoccupied bench. SEATS AND BENCHES BELONG THERETO FOR THE EXCLUSIVE USE OF THE GUESTS OF THE HOUSE.

What was permitted for her, a servant, a member of the staff? She'd have to find out before getting herself into trouble.

The pathway she trod cut between immaculately manicured lawns. To her left, couples played a game of croquet, laughing and bantering gaily. To her right, several women played lawn tennis in fancy garb. Didn't they swelter in their layers of clothing?

Several couples meandered along the same path as she, and alarm niggled her nerves. Was it acceptable for her to be there? She averted her eyes momentarily as a handsome young couple came near, but she couldn't help peeking as they passed.

"Do you know, darling, that there are four newlywed couples honeymooning here? Just like us." The pretty woman holding a pink parasol passed by her, eyes twinkling as she spoke to her new husband, oblivious to Addi's presence. "I guess it's because this resort is so romantic."

Addi sighed. Would she ever find love? She hoped so, for her greatest desire was to have a passel of children—and never again be alone. She'd been an only child, and when she was five, her mother died of a fever, leaving her papa and herself to fend for themselves. Their farm was a great distance from any of her schoolmates, so books became her dearest companions.

And nature. She'd spent many hours observing all that nature provided. Growing plants. Flying birds. Skittering field mice. Bugs and butterflies.

She'd painstakingly kept a journal of her observations. Studied them whenever she could. And, best of all, she got to read her papa's *Old Farmer's Almanac* from cover to cover every year.

The *Almanac* was a goldmine of information, featuring weather projections, nuances of all four seasons, planting charts, gardening tips, and fascinating astronomical data, such as the dates of the phases of the moon. But editor Robert Ware also provided interesting reading for the womenfolk such as recipes, articles on fashion, home economics, folklore, and so much more. She liked the scientific content better.

Papa chuckled every time he brought home the newest one and gingerly handed it to her. "Little Darlin', I'll be needing this back before the first thaw. Just you mind that."

She would kiss him on the cheek and promptly plop into her favorite chair. She'd devour the volume from cover to cover in the first week. Then she'd reread it several times thereafter.

Ah, Papa...if only you were here.

In the distance, a stringed quartet played on the veranda, pulling her from her meandering thoughts. She drew nearer, entranced by the beautiful music. The two violins, a viola, and a violoncello played a happy Celtic tune. She closed her eyes and imagined the instruments were children dancing around a maypole —in and out and around one another, skipping in the sunbeams and the gentle breeze.

But then, the music grew pensive, sad, and Addi could almost feel the tears and grief the strings produced, mirroring the thoughts of her papa.

Of her aloneness.

"Miss Bell? How providential. Aye, I was just going to deliver this missive to the hotel manager."

Mr. Donovan held a large manila envelope in his hand and waved it toward the massive edifice. "I had hoped I might find you and give you a tour of the hotel while I'm at it."

"Thank you, sir. I wasn't sure where I could go—or not—and I didn't want to break any rules. So yes, I'd be delighted to have a tour, so long as you also give me the rules of the place." She curtsied, relief...and excitement...quickening her pulse.

"Of course, miss. We wouldn't want you to get into any mischief unawares, would we?" Mr. Donovan chuckled.

Addi chuckled at his banter. "No sir. But may I ask, please? Does the quartet play every day? They are heavenly."

Mr. Donovan shrugged, slipping the envelope under his arm and rubbing his hands together. "There is often a morning concert, though not always the quartet. Sometimes, we have a military band. Other times, an ensemble of some sort. Still other times, there are various benefit concerts in one of the parlors. In the evening, the nine-piece Steubgen Orchestra plays waltzes and polkas and Germans and hops. And elegant balls now and then. Professor Frank Steubgen is the musical director. He composed a two-step number called 'The 1000 Island Souvenir March' that is now played all over the country. It's made him quite renowned."

"I love music and dancing, though I've enjoyed little of late." Addi smiled rather wistfully.

Mr. Donovan put a hand to his chin. "Aye, and though you can't participate in the concerts with the patrons, you can often hear the music from here. I come regularly to this very spot and take in the magic for I, too, love music of all kinds. Moreover, there are several fireworks displays throughout the summer for you to enjoy."

"Then I may join you here often—if I'm free, that is. What will my day look like, may I ask?" Addi bit her bottom lip, waiting for an answer.

The man's brow furrowed. "As I mentioned in my letter, you'll have charge of four-to-eight-year-olds from eight in the morning until five in the evening. Some evenings, you'll also care for a particular family's children, if requested. Otherwise, you're free in the evening, as long as you don't encroach on our patrons' privacy."

Addi clicked her tongue. "I never received a letter, sir. Mr. Sanderson is a neighbor and only informed me verbally that I had the position, and that I was to report to you today."

Mr. Donovan slapped the manila envelope on his thigh. "Blathers! No wonder you seemed so uninformed. I thought you might be a little simple-minded."

"I assure you, sir. I am not!" Addi huffed her indignation.

What other misconceptions might Mr. Donovan

have about her? And why did his opinions matter so much to her?

*L*iam bowed. "Excuse my assumption. Aye, I see you're a scrappy wee pluck of a thing who, indeed, has a sharp mind and an even sharper tongue. I meant no ill."

Miss Bell's scowl softened, but her glare remained. "Nor I, sir."

He averted her attention, pointing to the hotel. "Let's start here with a brief history. The Thousand Island House was finished in 1873, the year after President Grant visited the islands with George Pullman and thus began the amazing growth of the Thousand Islands. Colonel Orin G. Staples built the establishment in less than a year, and it's been a popular destination ever since."

Miss Bell put a thin finger to her chin. "I've heard of him. Didn't Colonel Staples start a medicine business in Watertown, sell it to someone in Albany, and build dozens of houses in the city with the profits?"

"Fifty-seven fine homes, to be exact. You have a keen memory. And just two years ago, he built the elegant Willard's Hotel in Washington, D.C."

"You don't say?" She studied the four-story hotel. "He certainly is a talented businessman, and this hotel is mighty grand."

He nodded. "Three-hundred-ninety-five rooms accommodate up to seven hundred guests, complete with family suites, a huge hundred-foot by forty-foot dining room, and a glorious six-hundred-and-twenty-four-foot grand promenade veranda."

"My, there must be an army of staff to serve so many guests." She put her hand to her chest.

He chuckled. "One hundred and fifty. Most are locals."

"But why is it named Thousand Island House without an *s* on Islands? Aren't there over eighteen hundred islands?"

He thought a moment. "I don't rightly know. Maybe to be different? You ask some crackin' good questions, miss. No wonder you're a teacher."

"Thank you, kind sir. I appreciate the complement." Miss Bell grinned.

They entered the hotel servants' area and passed through an enormous and modern kitchen. Liam warmly greeted everyone he met, whether servant or guest. They deserved no less.

He led the pretty lass up the staff stairs and stopped before entering the first-floor corridor, keeping his words barely above a whisper so as not to disturb any patrons. "I'll take you floor by floor, but we must be discreet."

"Of course, sir." She nodded, her dark eyes twinkling with excitement.

Opening the door to a wide hallway, he began his

tour. "On the first floor is the office, parlor, reception, reading rooms, bar, billiard room, telegraph office, barber shop, dining room, bathrooms and twenty-one guestrooms. You'll rarely, if ever, need to come here, but follow me, please, while I drop off this envelope."

On the way, Miss Bell's curiosity reminded him of a wee lassie in a sweets shop. She peeked into the luxurious common areas, gawked at the elaborate artwork, and discreetly glanced at the elegantly dressed patrons. No wonder she wanted to share all that boundless enthusiasm with the children.

As they passed room after room, he allowed her time to have a good look. And that gave him time to enjoy the delightful expressions on her pretty face.

After leaving the envelope with the office secretary, Liam led Miss Bell up to the second floor, but they didn't enter it. "Besides two reception rooms, private dining rooms, and a plethora of guestrooms, this floor also has a special wing that houses a huge public dining room with a twenty-seven-foot-high ceiling. Patrons, locals, and other vacationers are welcome to dine with us. Unfortunately, there's a luncheon going on, so you won't be able to see it today."

Her brow furrowed. "Such high ceilings, even higher than necessary for cooling purposes. Why?"

He shrugged, grasping for an answer. "The room seats several hundred guests. I expect that the high ceilings also disperse some of the noise."

"Oh, that's rather clever." She nodded.

"Aye. Not to mention, it looks quite grand." They climbed the stairs and stopped at the third-floor landing, where he again turned to his new employee. "The third and fourth floors are all parlors and guestrooms, but I want to show you the view of the river from the balcony. That is, if no guests are present."

When they arrived at the top floor and stepped onto the empty balcony, she gasped. "This is glorious! If I ignore the floor beneath my feet, I feel like an eagle soaring on the breeze."

Liam chuckled. "It's fortuitous no one is present, else you would have missed this sight." He drew near her and pointed west. "In that direction are Cherry Island, Friendly Island, St. Elmo Island, and Pullman Island. And to the east are the Cornwall Brothers docks and Hart Island in the distance."

She glanced at the docks, then pointed below. "And there's the pavilion. It looks rather small from here."

"It's not when you walk the breadth and width of it dozens of times a day. Or take care of little ones in it, I imagine." He chuckled, shrugging.

She snapped a determined nod at him. "I believe I shall enjoy my time here. Thank you for showing me the hotel, sir."

"Certainly. At least now you know where the children will stay when they're not with you." He waved a hand for her to retreat back into the servants' stairwell, and she immediately got the hint.

As he led her down the four floors, he continued

sharing pertinent—and hopefully interesting—information. "The hotel boasts modern electricity and plumbing. There's an elevator for patrons, and the accommodations are most luxurious. But we also have a wing for more modest clientele who come for fishing and boating. The Thousand Island House does not discriminate between the classes, and that's a unique feature of our hotel. The common fisherman and the wealthiest aristocrats from Watertown, Utica, New York City, Philadelphia, Pittsburg, Chicago, and elsewhere enjoy their holidays side by side."

"What a marvelous idea, but so unconventional." Miss Bell stopped on the bottom step and sighed.

Liam nodded as he opened the door to the outside, momentarily blinded by the bright sunshine. He shielded his eyes until they adjusted and peeked to see that she was doing the same. "Indeed. At night, eight hundred incandescent lamps illuminate the pathways, the shoreline, and the verandas."

She glanced at the nearby light pole. "It must look like a fairyland."

"Only the very best for our patrons, night and day. And there are always boats and fishing guides standing at the ready, seven days a week. At night, the grand steamer, the *St. Lawrence,* hosts searchlight tours. See? It's docked now." He pointed to the large white steamboat with a majestic eagle painted on its side. "Most sailings sell out weeks in advance."

Miss Bell drew in a deep breath. "She's a beauty. What's a searchlight tour?"

"The Folger brothers had her built in Clayton just last year. They included a one-million-candlepower searchlight atop its wheelhouse so they can conduct nighttime tours of the islands. I took one last month, and I must admit, it was a little eerie. A bit scary, but oh, so exhilarating."

The lovely lass shifted her weight from foot to foot, doe eyes dancing with excitement. "It sounds enchanting. I hope I can experience that one day."

Liam grinned. "Aye, I hope you can."

Perhaps with me?

What was he thinking? He could never encourage a flirtation with an employee. Such was strictly forbidden. But this was the first time he'd been tempted to.

CHAPTER 3

Addi ran her finger along the rim of the largest glass bowl she'd ever seen. She wrapped her arms around the circumference to measure it, barely touching the fingertips of one hand to the other. Where could such an enormous bowl have come from?

Mr. Donovan, of course. She'd but mentioned the request, and he promptly fulfilled it. Such a kind Irish gentleman. Not how she'd imagined an entertainment pavilion manager to be. She'd imagined her superior would be a large brusque man who led his workers like her superintendent, Mr. Wallace. She'd have to thank Mr. Donovan when she saw him.

And thank goodness, Mrs. Erving had found two smaller uniforms. She smoothed her skirts with a small smile before scurrying around her classroom, tidying anything amiss. Her first day needed to be above reproach.

She'd greet the children. Let them play. And later, lead them in charades so she could see their budding personalities at work.

The door opened, yanking Addi from her planning. She sucked in a reassuring breath, ready to tackle the adventures to come. Her first day at Thousand Island House nursery was about to begin.

A middle-aged woman entered, helped a chubby blond boy from the stroller she'd pushed, and shook her finger at him. "Be good for your teacher, Gregory. I will fetch you at five."

The boy stomped his foot, hands clenched. "I don't wanna be here. I wanna stay with you, Nanny."

"Father's orders, young man. Be good."

The nanny gave him a little push, exited briskly, and closed the door behind her without even talking to Addison.

Addi scurried to her new pupil's side. "Gregory, is it? Welcome. You're the first to arrive, so you have your choice of toys to play with."

The child glanced at the door and then across the room at the shelves filled with toys, puzzles, and books. His clear blue eyes sparkled with what she guessed might be mischief. He tipped his head. "Anything?"

She'd have to keep a sharp eye on that one. She grinned. "Yes. How old are you, child?"

The boy glared at her as if offended by her question. "Six—and *a half*." He snatched a tin drum with sticks off the shelf and banged it loudly just as a boy and girl tumbled into the classroom, trying to outrun one another.

"Beatcha."

The boy, a head smaller than his sister, beamed with pride. Both children wore plain, handmade clothes, their hair askew. Their shoes well-worn and scuffed.

Addi joined them. "Hello. And who might you be?"

The girl answered. "I'm Sally Jones and this is Markie. I'm almost seven and lost a tooth this morning. See?"

Sally displayed the gap in her teeth, but Markie interrupted her. "I just turned five last week. Pop made me a fishing pole. Ma is home with the sick baby."

"My, thank you for all that information. We will pray for the baby. Why don't you choose a toy or puzzle to play with?"

Addi pointed to the shelves, and lickety-split, the two hurried to make their choices.

Soon, a pretty young woman in a rich purple day dress entered, holding the hands of two little girls with sandy blond hair, light-brown eyes, thin lips, and pale skin who looked just like her. All three displayed expressions of angst, if not fear. Best to alleviate those fears from the onset.

"Welcome, ladies." Addi waved her arm toward the center of the room before putting out her hand to the woman. "I'm Miss Bell. I've been a teacher for five years and am happy to care for your little girls. And you are?"

The woman clung tighter to her girls, her eyes

flashing with worry. "Mrs. Simpson. These girls are Laura and Nora. They've never been apart from me."

Addi bent down and touched the girls' free hands, forming an intimate little circle. She spoke gently. "Are you twins?"

The slightly taller one shook her head. "I'm five. She's only four."

Their mother cleared her throat. "Irish twins."

"They are adorable, ma'am, and I'm sure we'll have a lovely time together." Addi smiled and stood, still holding their hands. "Please don't worry. I'll care for them as if they were my own."

Gregory banged the drum louder, seemingly demanding attention. She ignored him. For the moment. "Come, girls. Do you like puzzles? We have several."

Mrs. Simpson let go of the girls' hands and nudged them toward the toys, but Nora clung to her. "Go on, darling. I'll be back this afternoon to fetch you."

"They'll be fine, ma'am. Good day to you." Addi tugged them toward the other children.

After settling the girls to work on a farmyard puzzle together and checking on Sally and Markie, who were playing with blocks, she bid Gregory to find a quieter toy, steering him toward a wooden Noah's Ark full of tiny carved animals.

The boy folded his arms and pouted. "I want the drum." He smacked his hand on it and tried to yank it from her. "It's mine."

The four other children looked up from their play. Best to set expectations now.

She promptly set the drum on the top shelf, well out of reach, and patted his shoulder gently. "Let's save this for music time, young man. Can you match up the animals with their mates?"

"Of course I can." Gregory nodded, a tentative smile blossoming on his face.

Trouble averted.

For now.

Liam had observed the interchange with delight. He'd come to see if Miss Bell needed anything, but she obviously had things well in hand. He grinned at the scene. She'd handled the naughty lad rather deftly. Good to know. The previous nursery worker had lacked tact. Kindness, even.

Before he had a chance to address the lovely lass, the naval officer he'd met yesterday entered the room with a boy in a blue-and-white sailor suit, knickers to his knees and white socks under that. Liam cleared his throat to alert Miss Bell they were there, then addressed the pair, loud enough to draw the teacher's attention. "Welcome, Lieutenant Worthington. I didn't know you had a son. What's your name, young man?"

"Jimmy, sir."

The child saluted him. He was tall and thin, like his

father. His dark eyes and curly hair were his papa's too. A cute little cap completed his naval outfit.

Miss Bell joined them. She curtsied to the lieutenant as her cheeks turned pink. Then she held out her hand to the lad, and he took it with a grin. "Welcome, sir. Welcome, young man. Let's get you settled with the other children, shall we?"

Jimmy waved with his free hand as Miss Bell led him to the toys. "Farewell, Father. Have fun at the lighthouse."

Miss Bell sat the boy on the floor with a tin train set, checked on the other children still playing quietly, and returned to the men.

Lieutenant Worthington glanced at his boy. "Thank you, Miss Bell, for taking care of Jimmy. I'm off to inspect Sunken Rock Light. It's just offshore here in Alexandria Bay, so I should be back before end of day. There may be a few times, however, that I may not be back before day's end. Some lighthouses I am to inspect are a rather great distance from here."

"It's no problem, Lieutenant Worthington. I'd be happy to watch him anytime. That is, if it's all right with you, Mr. Donovan." Miss Bell shrugged, casting him a raised brow.

Liam grinned. "It's perfectly fine, miss. All part of your position. We aim to please."

"Very good. Thank you. Good day." Lieutenant Worthington tipped his hat.

Once the officer left, Miss Bell dipped a curtsy to

Liam. "Thank you, Mr. Donovan, for the beautiful bowl. It's perfect for a terrarium."

"You're welcome. It was collecting dust on the upper kitchen shelves. A leftover from a wedding a few years ago. Chef McClelland said you could keep it."

Miss Bell fairly glowed. "Please tell the chef thank you. We will enjoy it all summer long. I can't wait to take the children out hunting for treasures to fill it. Do you suppose there might be a piece of cheesecloth we could use too?"

"Whatever for?"

Would she ask for something new every time he saw her? The woman could prove rather vexing if she kept this up.

She smiled, her eyebrows rising too. "After we establish the terrarium plants, I'd like to turn it into an insectarium and keep live insects for the children to observe. Beetles, ants, worms, grasshoppers, caterpillars. That sort of thing. We'd need to cover the terrarium so the bugs don't get out, but they also need air to breathe. The cheesecloth will help with that."

"You're quite the wee scientist, Miss Bell. I shall see what I can procure." Liam chuckled. A valid reason. He'd find her the cheesecloth if he had to buy it himself.

Miss Bell waved her hands in front of her. "No hurry, sir. It will be a week or more before we collect critters."

Little Laura joined them, tugging on Miss Bell's

skirt. "That boy is teasing Sally and Markie. He says they don't belong here 'cuz they're poor folk. He made Sally cry. But I like them, ma'am, so please make him stop."

"I like them too. Excuse me, Mr. Donovan, but I must attend to this immediately." Miss Bell's dark eyes grew stormy, and she bit her bottom lip.

"Aye. Carry on, then."

Liam stepped out the door but left it ajar so he could hear how she would deal with the situation. He even peeked in to watch. After all, he had to be sure his employee would manage the guests' children well.

Miss Bell took Gregory's hand and led him to the teary Sally and her brother. She squatted down to their level, speaking gently. "What's going on here, young man?"

Gregory stared at the floor and said nothing. Sally sniffed back her tears. Markie rolled a wooden wagon on the table, his eyes sad. She pressed the potential troublemaker to answer her. "Were you unkind, Gregory?"

The laddie's head popped up. "They *are* poor folk. Look at their clothes. And their shoes. I didn't do nothing wrong."

"It doesn't matter what a person wears. It matters if the person behaves and is kind. That is unkind, Gregory. Say you're sorry, please." Miss Bell's tone was firm, but her face shone compassion.

Gregory pasted his lips together and shook his head.

She glanced at all the children who were now watching to see what she'd do. She repeated her instruction, a bit stronger. "You will not be unkind in my classroom. Say you are sorry, *now*, or you'll sit in the corner."

Gregory folded his arms. "Mother says I shouldn't play with poor folk, or I might catch their bugs."

Miss Bell let out a puff of air that blew the boy's hair back from his forehead. Then she groaned, took Gregory's hand, and nearly dragged him to the far corner of the room. "They do not have bugs, young man, and saying so is rude. At the Thousand Island House, we welcome people from all walks of life, from every class, of any age. We do not discriminate, and we *will* be respectful to everyone. When you are ready to be kind, you can join us. Until then, sit here." She placed a chair facing the corner and sat Gregory in it. Then she touched his shoulders gently. "I know you can be a good boy if you try."

Miss Bell returned to the other children, but on the way, she caught Liam watching her.

"Well done, miss. Carry on." He whispered his encouragement, but his face burned as he closed the door.

*A*ddi welcomed Gert into the classroom and took the large tray laden with sandwiches, carrot sticks, and fat glasses of milk. Upon further inspection, there were even gingersnaps for a later snack. "Thank you, Gert, for the lunch. It's very kind of you to bring it."

Gert huffed, scrunching up her pudgy face into a most unbecoming frown. "Don't thank me. I ain't your slave, miss. I was up at five, while you slept the day away. I work my hands to the bone until past seven at night. It's Chef who has me dragging this over here every day, else you'd be getting your own food for them rug rats."

"I'm sorry, miss." She sighed at the vehemence of her roommate.

Gert folded her arms over her ample chest. "You've got a highbrow position, that's for sure, sittin' around here while them children occupy themselves. Sleeping in half the morning and done by five. It ain't fair, I say."

Buxom, brazen, and obviously bitter, the woman turned on her heel and fled the room before Addi had the chance to smooth her rumpled feathers. In lieu of calming her would-be friend, she tossed up a quick prayer that Gert would find peace in her situation, if not friendship with her.

"I'm hungry." Gregory whined. "I wanna eat."

"Me too." Nora nodded. "We didn't get breakfast."

Addi settled the children at the table and gave them

their meal. While they ate, she encouraged her young charges to talk about their families, their parents, their homes. Sally and Markie lived with their grandparents on a humble farm. The others had fine homes in Buffalo, Syracuse, and Albany.

When they finished lunch, it was time to play charades. All but Gregory knew how to play, so Addi started the game with simple words such as *ear, blink, spin, cold, cry*, and *sneeze*. The children laughed, guessed well, and enjoyed the fun. She observed the confidence of Jimmy, the sisterly love of Laura and Nora, and the reticence of Sally and Markie.

And Gregory? For all his puffed-up superiority, the child seemed lonely and unsure of himself.

As Markie comically acted out the word *baby* by sucking on an imaginary bottle and burping loudly, her class became rather raucous until Mr. Donovan entered the room, displeasure evident by the scowl on his handsome face.

Addi tried to hush the children, but their enthusiasm kept them laughing and playing. She finally calmed them down and engaged them in a whisper game.

Only then did she join the pavilion manager at the door. "I'm sorry about that. They were having far too much fun."

Mr. Donovan shrugged. "Aye, I don't want to knock the wind out of your bagpipes, miss, but you simply have to keep the noise down. We have patrons here who are complaining."

She glanced back at the children, who were whispering and giggling quietly. "Charades is a great way to get to know the children. They were having so much fun, and I was learning so much about them, I forgot about the noise. Forgive me, sir."

"You light up like a firefly when you speak of the children. It's quite a heartening sight." Mr. Donovan's eyes twinkled, and a wide smile crossed his lips.

"They're precious children, all, but they are young and need to expend their excess energy, especially after lunch. Perhaps I should take them outside and let them run it off."

Mr. Donovan glanced at the group before shaking his head. "There's not much room on this tiny island for children to run freely, and you may do so only when adult patrons are not meandering around. It's probably best to take them to the mainland, but be careful when you cross over the bridge. We don't want any little ones falling into the river."

Addi nodded. "Of course, sir. I will protect them with my life."

As if my future depended on it. Didn't it?

A seed of trepidation took root. Perhaps she'd wait a few days for this adventure. Meanwhile, she could convince herself she was capable of guarding the lives of six small individuals on her own.

CHAPTER 4

In just three days, Addi had already learned a boatload about her small charges. Their strengths and weakness. Their fears and frustrations. And more. All she need do was pay attention to their words and deeds.

Easy as catching a turtle in the grass.

Before the children arrived on Thursday, the fourth morning her of new job, she carefully printed a saying on the chalkboard in her best printing: *Praise the young and they will flourish.—an Irish Proverb.* Instead of a dot over the I's, she drew little hearts. She loved that saying and tried to live by it, especially when she was caring for precious little lives like these six children.

Gregory reminded her of a lost soul. He tended to be a bully—not because he was ill-willed but because he'd been taught to be cruel. From the things he said, his mother and father were narrow-minded, prejudiced, and thought much too highly of themselves. It was beyond her imagination how she could speak to this. For now, she'd praise him when he was good and hope for the best.

Jimmy, a bit mollycoddled, showed extraordinary leadership and empathy for others. Though Gregory teased him incessantly about his sailor suit, which he wore daily, the lieutenant's son didn't flinch. Her task, she decided, was to help him become a confident leader.

The others just wanted to be loved and have fun, and though each differed greatly from the other, their eagerness to learn and grow thrilled her to her toes.

When all six of her children finally arrived and settled into the room for the day, she presented her plan. "Today we are going to be scientists and create a terrarium. Does anyone know what that means?"

Laura spoke up. "A scientist is someone who studies things to learn about it."

"Very good, Laura. And what is a terrarium?" Addi clapped her hands.

All six pairs of eyes stared at her blankly.

She set the large glass bowl in front of the children. "A terrarium is a place where we can grow plants and, perhaps, keep some bugs, worms, turtles, or frogs in it later on. This will be our terrarium. I've already collected these small stones for the bottom layer, but we will add much more to our science experiment. That way, we can study the plants and critters like real scientists by watching them grow and learning about them."

"Can we keep a snake in there too?" Gregory raised his hand while belting out his question.

She swallowed hard and shook her head. "Some terrariums might hold snakes, but ours will not."

She could handle almost every other creature *but* snakes. They terrified her, ever since her neighbor, Stu, stuck a huge writhing one in her bed when she was four.

The children wiggled and giggled with excitement, so she continued explaining her plan. "This morning, we will go onto the mainland and look for moss, rich, dark soil, and small plants. But you must promise me something."

Several of the children murmured, "What?"

"When we cross over the river, you must be very careful not to fall in."

She grinned, studying their reactions.

Markie raised his hand and waited for her to acknowledge him. "Papa tells us that every day. He said we'd get a whoopin' if we fell in and two if we pushed anyone into the water."

"Your papa is wise to warn you. We must always respect water. It can be our friend, but it can also be dangerous. So...when we cross the river or search the shore, let's stay dry, okay?"

Six little voices said, "yes, ma'am," almost in unison.

She handed Gregory a pot and Markie a small

bucket. "Can you boys carry these for us?" The boys nodded. Then she gave Sally and Nora little wicker baskets. "For the plants." Finally, she handed petite hand shovels to Laura and Jimmy and picked up a pair of sheers, slipping them into her apron pocket. "Ready?"

The children lined up two-by-two as instructed, and Addi reminded them again to behave and be safe. Like obedient little soldiers, her troop followed her silently through the pavilion, out the back door, and over the dock-bridge between Casino Island and the Thousand Island House hotel property. Once safely across, she breathed a sigh of relief.

"Well done, children. Now let's find our terrarium contents."

For the next hour, Addi led the group to find all they needed to create a beautiful terrarium, explaining what each thing was and why they required it. They took turns shoveling soil into Markie's bucket. They carefully gathered soft green moss and slipped it into Gregory's pot. Then they filled the girls' baskets with small plants, including clover, tiny ferns, and wild violets. They even collected a handful of shells, twigs, and colorful pebbles.

Several times, one or the other asked to keep a bug or two, but Addi declined. "We need to establish the plants first and get a sheet of cheesecloth to cover the terrarium. Otherwise, the bugs will get out and die in the room."

Before returning to the classroom, she let the children play The Farmer in the Dell. Markie was the farmer and chose his sister, Sally, to be his wife. Sally chose Nora to be her child, and Nora chose Jimmy to be her dog.

But Gregory taunted Jimmy under his breath. "Yeah, you're a dog all right. Why don't you run away and howl at the moon?"

Addi slipped in beside him while Jimmy chose Laura to be the cat. "Gregory, you're being unkind again. You need to apologize to Jimmy."

Before Gregory had the chance say he was sorry, Laura picked him to be the mouse, and he selected Miss Bell to be the cheese. Everyone laughed happily when the game was done, and she smiled when Gregory leaned into Jimmy and said one word. "Sorry."

It was enough. For now.

Suddenly, a group of older children ran in front of them and stopped to stare. Their leader, a tall, lanky man with dark hair and droopy eyes, swaggered up to her and put out his hand. He popped his gum loudly. "Melvin Olson. I keep these older children in line and occupied. You can call me Mel."

She shook it. "I'm Addi. Pleased to meet you."

Mel scanned her class and popped his gum again. "Sorry, but this is our turf. You'd better move along, or one of these *nursery* kids might get hurt."

She stiffened her back. How rude. "I didn't realize this area was out of bounds to us."

"It is when we're here. I teach the big kids all sorts of sports, not just nursery games." *Snap. Crack. Pop.*

She'd heard enough. "Excuse me, but this is a free country, and I wasn't informed of your exclusive use of this grassy knoll. Good day." She turned on her heel and addressed her children. "Come, we have a terrarium to create."

Without looking back, she led her class over the bridge and into the room, where lunch awaited them.

After they ate, Addi and the children carefully constructed their terrarium, layering the gravel, soil, and moss, then adding plants, shells, and sticks to form a perfect little creation. "We only need to water it once a month or so because the moss and plants create their own little world by putting moisture into the air. In a week or two, we'll see what critters we can add to that world."

Rather like what she was doing this summer with the children—creating their own world. One where they could all be comfortable and happy. With any luck, this would indeed be the best summer ever.

*L*iam had been waiting all morning to check in on Miss Bell. He'd been to her room twice and both times found it empty. And he'd left her a gift, a piece of cheesecloth he'd bought himself.

The first time, he'd met Mel in the hallway, popping

his gum and joking loudly with his group of children in a most uncouth way. Before the day's end, he'd have to deal with that lad and set him upon a proper path—for both of their sakes.

The second time, he found the kitchen maid Gert snooping around Miss Bell's classroom. She'd brought their lunch, and after making a silly excuse about searching for napkins, she batted her gray, sad eyes at him as he escorted her out of the pavilion and sent her back to the kitchen.

The woman was insufferable.

Suddenly, the laughter of small children entering from the back door followed by their caregiver caught his attention.

"Shhh...quiet in the hallway. Remember?" Miss Bell scurried them along as they headed to their room. "Hush, or we'll get in trouble."

When they passed him, Liam smiled. "Good afternoon, Miss Bell. Children. I wondered if you'd jumped ship and sailed away."

Jimmy spoke. "We didn't get on a ship, sir. The docks here aren't big enough for a ship. Only for a steamer or smaller boat." He glanced at his teacher. "We had lunch, then we went for a walk in the garden."

Liam chuckled at the child's boat knowledge, shared in such a serious manner. "That's true. I only meant... Never mind. So you've already eaten?"

"We have." Miss Bell touched Laura's shoulder.

"Children, please thank Mr. Donovan for the glass bowl. And thanks, too, for the cheesecloth."

All six children murmured their thanks.

"If you'll excuse us, sir, we should get back to the classroom." The lovely lass bobbed a curtsy.

He snapped a nod. "Aye, forgive me for interrupting you."

Miss Bell smiled before hurrying to catch up with her children, speaking over her shoulder. "Come and see the terrarium later on. It will please the children to show you."

"I will. Thank you. Carry on, then." Liam grinned at the warm invitation.

A few hours later, he could wait no longer. Peals of laughter and song wafted down the hallway. Joyful but too noisy. How could he help Miss Bell understand she needed to keep the children quiet? Her elderly predecessor ruled the children with a rod of iron, so he'd barely heard a peep from them when they were in the old woman's care. Yet Miss Bell's group seemed so much happier under her amiable oversight. How to balance the two?

"Who has stolen my watch and chain?"

Ah, they were playing London Bridge. He entered the room, interrupting their fun. "Good afternoon, children."

"You wanna play with us?" Markie stopped leading the march, almost causing the others to crash into him.

"Aye, young man. Thank you for the invitation." Liam nodded.

Miss Bell's chocolate eyes twinkled with delight. "Please do. Perhaps you and I should be the bridge since we're taller than these fine folks?"

After she spoke, Miss Bell's eyes flashed alarm. She bit her lip and took a quivering breath, as if she wanted to take back her invitation. Did she think it improper to build a bridge with him, or did she not want him to join the fun?

Sally and Laura quickly gave up their spots as the bridge and joined the line of children. Tentatively, Liam took Miss Bell's hands. When he touched her, warmth like hot maple syrup drifted up his arm and straight to his heart. It skipped at least four beats before pounding out a happy rhythm inside his chest.

When he glanced at Miss Bell, pink cheeks bloomed on her pretty face. Then she smiled and sang in a lovely soprano voice.

The children joined her song, marching round and round the two of them until, on the word *lady,* Miss Bell and he lowered their arms, caught hold of Nora, and shook her playfully while she giggled with glee. They repeated the song over and over until each child had the chance to be caught by them. When it was done, Liam didn't want it to end, and he understood why so much mirth floated down the hallway from this room.

"Thank you, Mr. Donovan, for being a splendid

bridge. Would you like to see our terrarium?" Miss Bell curtsied to him, her eyes sparking delight, maybe more?

He nodded. "Please. Show me what have you made, children."

Gregory and Jimmy took his hands and led him to the table. Dirt, moss, and pebbles littered the floor and table, but they had transformed the bowl into a small wonderland.

Sally pointed to it. "This is our terrarium. We're gonna study it, and then we'll find some bugs and worms so they can live in there."

"That's a fine idea." Liam chuckled. "Maybe you can add a tiny fairy or two. But you have to catch them carefully, by their wings, so they won't fly away."

"Really? Where can we find one?" Nora's eyes grew wide.

Miss Bell cleared her throat. "He's kidding, Nora. We'll find some critters for our terrarium next week, just you mind that."

Liam shrugged. "Sorry to confuse the wee lassie. Thank you for the game and view of the lovely terrarium. And please be sure to clean this mess up before you finish your day."

A groan slipped past Miss Bell's lips, followed by a spark in her narrowed eyes. She pressed her lips together for a moment before speaking. "Messes are just a part of the process with little ones. But yes, of course, I'll clean the room before I'm done."

Her exasperation was all too evident, as if their own

bridge had fallen down. How easy it was to offend without even realizing it. Better to say nothing about the noise. "Good day to you, children. Miss Bell. Carry on, then."

Leaving the room, Liam nearly bumped into Mel.

Pop. Smack. "Hey, Mr. Donovan. How's your day going?"

"Fine. Where are the children?"

Mel shoved his gum into the side of his cheek. "They're reading. I give them quiet time every afternoon. Gives me a chance to catch my breath."

Now would be a good time to speak to him. But how? "Do you have a minute to talk?"

Pop. "Sure, boss. What's up?"

Liam pointed to his mouth. "*That's* the problem. Listen, Mel. I know ballplayers like to chew gum, but it's not appropriate at such a fine resort as the Thousand Island House. Please, stop chewing gum while you're working or when you are on the property. It sets a poor example for the children, and it's an irritation to many. Please refrain from the habit immediately."

Mel took a step back as if he'd been slapped. "Really, boss? I had no idea." *Pop.*

Liam let out a long, low groan to punctuate his position. "Chewing, popping, cracking, and snapping your gum is a rude habit. It's distracting and unprofessional, and no one wants to hear the smacking and popping sounds. Please stop it at once. When you're off the property on your day off, you may do as you please, as long as you are not with patrons."

Pop. "Okay, boss. But it won't be an easy habit to break. Say, what's with the nursery worker? She's rather rude, don't you think?"

Liam pointed to his mouth. "Out. Now. Please." He waited until Mel removed the gum from his mouth and wrapped it in a piece of paper Mel pulled from his pocket before continuing. "Why do you say Miss Bell is rude?"

In the absence of gum, Mel popped his lips. Speaking of rude. "She got in a snit when I asked her to leave so we could use the ball field. She was playing some silly nursery game with those babies."

"Mel, you don't have exclusive use of the field. There's an Irish proverb that says, 'A silent mouth never did any harm.' Maybe you should take that to heart, lad."

Mel shoved his hands in his pockets. "Perhaps I should."

Liam turned away, dismissing the young man.

If only he could dismiss his growing feelings for the nursery teacher.

CHAPTER 5

Torrential rain nearly soaked Addi through as she scurried from the boarding house to the pavilion. Not even the large black umbrella Mrs. Erving lent her kept her skirts dry. It would likely be a long, Noah day of dark skies and grouchy children. No telling how many patrons would even bother to bring their children out on such a stormy day.

As she did every day, Addi wrote a saying on the chalkboard. *Bricks and mortar make a house—or a classroom—but the laughter of children makes a home—or a class. — An Irish proverb.* She loved starting the day with a prayer and an inspiring quote they could talk about.

Since Laura and Nora didn't come, Addi guided the four remaining children in learning a table game or two. Gregory and Sally played checkers, and the boy was delighted to win, jumping up and down and whooping so loudly that Addi had to calm him. Markie and Jimmy played dominoes quietly and amiably, laughing and talking like old friends.

Once the games ended, she read the Irish proverb and led them in a discussion about building a house on a firm foundation. She read Matthew 7:24-25 to them. "Jesus said, 'Therefore, whosoever heareth these sayings of mine, and doeth them, I will liken him unto a wise man, which built his house upon a rock. And the rain descended, and the floods came, and the winds blew, and beat upon that house; and it fell not: for it was founded upon a rock.'"

The children listened quietly until Jimmy raised his hand. "It's like the three little pigs. One built his house with straw, and it fell. One with sticks, and it fell. But the one who built his house with bricks, it didn't fall, and he was safe. They build most lighthouses on rock and make them of bricks, so the storms can't blow them down."

Addi swallowed her amazement. "Well, young man. I couldn't have said it better myself. Thank you for that. Now, let's act out the three little pigs. Who wants to be the wolf?"

"I do!" Gregory jumped up.

Of course, he did. "All right, but any wolf in my classroom cannot break anything or hurt anyone. Is that clear?"

The child rolled his eyes but agreed. "I'll just pretend."

Once the children acted out the fable, Addi turned

their attention to a quieter game, showing them how to use a teetotum. "This wooden top has numbers along the side. See? When we spin it, it will fall on one side. The number facing up is the number of moves you can make along the game board. We use it instead of dice."

Markie scrunched up his face. "Ma says gambling and playing with dice is a sin."

What was she to say to that? Nothing. Instead, she placed a game box in front of them. The cover showed an intricately bedecked elephant with scenes of the game on its back.

"Father and I play Elephant and Castle all the time." Jimmy clapped his hands.

Addi smiled. "Then you can help us all learn how to play. Its full name is The Noble Game of Elephant and Castle, or Traveling in Asia. Do you know where Asia is, children?"

Sally raised her hand. "India and China are in Asia. My uncle is a missionary there."

"That's right. Well done, Sally. What a clever girl you are."

Sally's grin lit the room.

Addi tapped the box and grinned. "Who wants to play?"

All four children shot up eager hands. Each child took a colored traveler pawn. For the next hour, Addi guided her young charges through a grand tour of northern Russia, China, India, and Japan on an ornate board depicting an elephant and Indian guide during the height of the British Empire. She helped them spin the teetotum and count the number of spaces to move. Then she read the description in the rule book that described different scenes from Asia, adapting it to make it easy for her little ones to understand. When Markie made it home first, all but Gregory congratulated him. He, on the other hand, scowled and pouted.

Addi diverted the children's attention. "Why don't each of you play on your own until lunch? There's a yo-yo, whirligig, finger top, bilbo catcher, and jumping jack man. But play quietly, please."

She turned to the still-pouting boy and patted his shoulder, bending down to whisper comfort. "Part of being kind is being a good sport, Gregory. It really doesn't matter who wins a game. It's how you respond that counts."

"But I wanted to win. Ma and Pa always let me win, even when I don't." The little boy stuck his bottom lip out.

She cast him a questioning shrug. "Is that really winning?"

"No, but it feels better than losing. Can I go and play with the jumping jack man now?"

Addi grinned and handed him the jointed toy that used strings to move its arms and legs. "It just happens that Jack is waiting for you."

"Thank you, Miss Bell." Gregory smiled as he took the toy.

She ruffled his hair lovingly. "You're quite welcome, young man."

A quarter of an hour later, Gert knocked on the door and let herself in. A tea towel covered the lunch tray, and a scowl covered her face. Raindrops dripped from her bonnet.

Addi rushed to her side and took the tray. "I'm so sorry you had to come out on a day like this. Can I get you a towel?"

Gert cast her a narrow-eyed glare, but before she could answer, Mr. Donovan stepped into the room and handed the kitchen maid a towel. "I saw you come in from the rain, miss, and thought you could use this."

"Sure is a blustery day." She wiped her hair, dress, and face with the towel before handing it back to Mr. Donovan. "Glad I don't got to come back here today."

Addi counted seven bowls of stew. "There are two extra meals since Laura and Nora didn't come. Care to join us for lunch, Mr. Donovan? Gert?"

Gert gawked at Mr. Donovan and he at Addi. Both shrugged simultaneously.

"I suppose I can stay for a few minutes." Gert nodded.

Mr. Donovan pulled back a chair. "Me too. It's a quiet day here at the pavilion."

Addi settled the children at one end of the table and the adults at the other, each with a bowl of stew and glasses of milk. After she asked Mr. Donovan to say a blessing, they enjoyed their meal.

Gert slurped her stew. "Mighty hearty beef stew on a blustery day. But it's too salty, if you ask me."

"It's very good. Did you make it?" Mr. Donovan arched a brow at her.

Gert shook her head. "I make the breads and assist the hotel's chef. He's a famous chef, you know."

"Yes, I knew that. We hire only the best staff possible." He grinned, casting a tender smile at Addi instead.

Gert's gaze darted from Mr. Donovan to Addi. Back and forth until the gaze turned to a glare. At Addi. The maid harrumphed, and she hoisted herself to standing, her stew unfinished. "I must be on my way."

"Thanks again for bringing this delicious meal. See you tonight." Addi stood, too, and walked her to the door.

Gert snorted. "Not if I can help it."

Why was Gert so prickly? And did she detect jealousy? Was Gert smitten with Mr. Donovan? Though Addi would like to form a friendship with the woman, every time she thought she'd made some headway with the her, it was two steps back. Would it never change?

*L*iam took his time eating the stew. Just being near Miss Bell brought a ray of sunshine into his otherwise stormy day. The few patrons who had ventured out into the weather to visit the pavilion were as gloomy as the sky above. Besides dealing with grumpy patrons, he'd had to remind Melvin—again—to refrain from chomping on his gum. And now the kitchen maid's surly disposition cast a pall over lunch. Good riddance.

Miss Bell excused herself to check on the children. After wiping a spill that the smallest boy had made, she returned to their end of the table.

"Sorry. The children really are darlings but a bit messy at times. We've been playing table games, and this afternoon, I'll teach them some more."

He wiped his mouth on his napkin. "You needn't work so hard. You are expected only to care for these children, not to amuse them every moment."

"Oh, I just love entertaining and training and teaching them. It's not a bother. Really." Her eyes twinkled delight.

He chuckled. "Your boundless energy matches that of a four-year-old boy who's been in grandma's cookie jar far too often."

"I suppose." She giggled. "They energize me with their inquisitiveness and desire to learn."

He glanced around the room. Toys scattered on the floor. The expensive board game just waiting to be trampled underfoot. "Perhaps you can teach them to pick up after themselves? That's a costly game."

She glanced in the direction of his gaze and swallowed hard. "Oh, I am sorry. I had meant to take care of that but got distracted."

When she stood to do just that, he grasped her

hand. Warmth shot up his arm, and her eyes grew wide. A pretty pink colored her cheeks.

"Finish your meal, miss. The game can wait."

He took a final bite of his stew, giving himself time to gather his courage. "Before I go, may I invite you on an evening stroll, if the rain stops?"

Miss Bell blinked. Then she licked her lips. "Perhaps. If the storm passes."

"Aye. Thanks for lunch." Liam stood, a victorious grin pulling his face taut. "Until the raindrops stop, then."

Before she could decline his invitation, he waved to the children and fled the room.

Hours later, the rain had stopped, and the sun shone brightly. It'd be a crackin' evening to stroll with Miss Bell. Something about her drew him to want to know what made her tick. Why did children fill her soul with joy? Why was she so charmingly inquisitive about the world around her? What were her goals in life?

He caught her on the way out of her classroom and waved the picnic basket he'd procured. Hopefully, it would entice her to enjoy an alfresco dinner with him. "It's nothing fancy. Fried chicken. Potato salad. And carrot cake."

"Sounds wonderful. But is it proper? You being my superior, I mean." Miss Bell giggled, the sound tickling his insides.

"We're both off work. Just two colleagues having dinner. Right?"

"I suppose. I just don't want to get in trouble with Mrs. Erving." She chewed her lip.

He waved off her concern. "Oh, she's more bark than bite. 'Sides, how's she to know? We can eat here on the island and then take a leisurely stroll around the hotel."

She agreed, and they enjoyed their picnic on the shore of the St. Lawrence. While they ate, a huge freighter sailed past them, and Miss Bell put her hand to her chest. "It never ceases to amaze me how big those ships are. Whether lakers or salties, they're larger than many of these islands and they make me feel very small."

"Small, but mighty, I reckon." Liam winked at her. "I see how deftly you deal with naughty children and command the respect of all of them. I made a stellar hire when I took old Mr. Sanderson's recommendation."

"Thank you, kind sir." Miss Bell grinned, pleasure blossoming on her pretty face. "I learned so much about children in my five years as school mistress at the Watertown Center School. Since it was a one-room schoolhouse, I taught children from ages five to sixteen, which makes this position a breeze. And what about you? How long have you been here?"

He gazed at the billowy clouds dancing on the breeze. "Just three years now. Before that, I worked at the Woodruff Hotel in Watertown. Know of it?"

She gave a soft laugh. "Do I! Papa took me there once, for a concert. He told me that Susan B. Anthony and President Ulysses S. Grant stayed there."

"Many famous people stayed there. With the train station just behind the hotel, folks from New York City and other places downstate would stop there on the way to their Thousand Islands summer homes. Many said it rivaled the Waldorf Astoria."

"It was an epic experience for me, to be sure. And, I have to admit, this Thousand Island House is equally wonderful."

"Shall we explore its wonder? I hear the Steubgen Orchestra is playing on the veranda tonight."

Her eyes twinkling, she nodded and promptly packed up the picnic. They dropped the basket at the back door, crossed the tiny bridge, and soon heard the music dancing on the breeze.

Liam took a risk, offering her his arm as they sauntered toward the music. His chest swelled simply to have her there. He cleared his throat and took another risk. "I know it's only been ten days since we met, but I'd like you to call me Liam when no one else is around. Would that suit you?"

"And you can call me Addi. When no one else is around." She smiled, squeezing his arm.

"I thought your name is Addison? Addi is a nickname?"

"It is." As they approached the far end of the veranda, she surveyed the fine décor, her eyes dancing with delight. "How lovely. But why so much gilt, even on the veranda's chairs and decorations? And I recall much more inside."

He chuckled. "Did you know that Mark Twain coined the term *Gilded Age* in his 1873 novel *The Gilded Age: A Tale of Today* to satirize the era of social problems masked by a layer of thin gold gilding? I read the book last year and found it to be a fascinating expose of our times, even of the growth happening here in these Thousand Islands. And journalists are using that very term more and more every day."

Addi nodded. "I know that the growth of this area began when President Grant visited Mr. Pullman when I was just a child."

"Aye. It began in 1872 when the wealthy came and scooped up the islands to build lavish summer homes, mansions, and castles. We are living in a time of economic growth and innovation. Did you know that a half-million patents were issued for new inventions in the past decade or so, including hundreds by Thomas Edison, George Eastman, Westinghouse, among others?"

She gasped. "I wasn't aware of that. Such brilliant minds."

He actually knew something the clever lass didn't? He grinned. "Thomas Edison's Menlo Park laboratory is researching and developing marvels of all kinds, including the phonograph, carbon telephone transmission, and electric lights. Thanks to inventions such as delivery of electric power, the world is becoming brighter, safer, more convenient and comfortable, and all around better. Unfortunately, it also has its ills, and too often the rich get richer, and the poor get poorer. I hope that changes one day."

Addi waved an arm toward the hotel. "Ah, but so much change brings places like this and people like me who get to work here. Those electric lights in my classroom are a wonder, especially on rainy days."

"Aye, that's what I enjoy about you, Miss...Addi. You're so interested in things most women would find uninteresting."

Just saying her name sent chills up his spine.

And set his heart to pound. Dare he hope she might be interested in *him*?

CHAPTER 6

usic from the Steubgen Orchestra drew Addi's attention from Liam's eloquent words. Though she found the information interesting and delighted in his melodic Irish lilt, she wanted to indulge in the lovely music floating in the warm evening air.

"Can we listen to the music for a little while, please?"

Liam grinned an apology. "Of course, my dear. I jabber on all too often. Follow me."

My dear? The only other person who called her that was her papa. The term of endearment sent shivers down her spine. Was he interested in her as more than a friend? Surely not. Still, if she was honest, her heart ticked up a bit whenever he came her way. She'd even dreamed about him once.

Like little children sneaking to glimpse Santa, she

and Liam stealthily rounded the corner of the hotel veranda and stood near a clump of lilacs, hidden from the view of patrons but close enough to hear the music clearly. Though the blossoms had nearly faded, their scent still had Addi stifling a sneeze. Most likely, the late-winter snowstorms had pushed back their blossoming time, else they'd all be gone by now. Her chest tightened as their intoxicating scent reminded her of the lilacs her mother had so carefully tended while still alive. The memory made her happy and sad at the same time.

Turning her attention to the music, Addi detected the three-four time signature of a Viennese waltz. She leaned in to whisper to Liam, and the musky scent of his aftershave mixed with the lilacs most pleasantly. "I've heard this before. At the Woodruff."

Liam nodded. "Aye, 'tis lovely, but my favorite is a good reel."

Addi squeezed his arm, imagining him twirling her about 'till she was dizzy. She'd never danced a reel, but with him, it would be a pleasure. And to hear live music in person, here? In the open air? With him? Well, this was magical.

What was happening to her? The thought made her tummy flip-flop, and her hands grew clammy. She swallowed her angst. Mrs. Erving said she was not to fraternize with men, either staff or patrons. She could lose her job.

She snuck a guilty glance at Liam, whose eyes were

closed, a gentle smile on his lips. So handsome. And kind. Her only friend there at the Thousand Island House hotel. In all of Alexandria Bay, for that matter.

"Good evening, Mr. Donovan. Miss Bell. This is enchanting music on a lovely evening, is it not?"

Lieutenant Worthington tipped his sailor cap. Still in uniform, as always, the lieutenant was a striking man to behold. Stunning, really. But he never smiled. Not even when he brought little Jimmy to class and said goodbye to his young son. And not now.

Addi curtsied. "Good evening to you, sir. Yes. It's a lovely night, now that the storm has passed."

Liam nodded, snapping into his managerial role. "Sir. May I get you a chair? A drink?"

Lieutenant Worthington shook his head. "I'm fine. I'd rather stand, thank you, and no drink for me. I never imbibe."

"Very good. Are you enjoying your stay at the hotel?" Liam turned his full attention to the Navy man, as if she wasn't there.

"Indeed, I am. And Jimmy adores his teacher."

The lieutenant fastened his deep-set eyes on her until the need to smooth her hair became overpowering. He continued to stare at her for several more moments with no sign of emotion, good or bad. As if he were examining a portrait, or a ship. Then a tiny spark lit his gaze, but it went out just as quickly as it had come. She tried to decipher the meaning of his few words and what he was thinking, but without success.

Did he feel the same as his son, or was there something else going on behind the stalwart military façade?

Liam broke the silence, turning the lieutenant's gaze from her—thank goodness. "I enjoyed lunch with the nursery class today and find Miss Bell to be a fine teacher. All the children seem to love her."

Though he spoke about her, he didn't look at her. In fact, he angled his shoulders away from her, as if to block her. Was he embarrassed? Attempting to avoid any scandal? Either way, the shunning pricked Addi's heart.

"Indeed." The lieutenant's gaze flicked back in her direction.

Liam, however, still didn't look at her. "How are your lighthouse inspections going? Will they take all summer?"

Addi stepped back into the shadows. Being ignored always heightened her profound sense of aloneness. It created an ache that went to her core and made her feel small. Insignificant. Unimportant. And Liam ignoring her hurt even more. Perhaps she should slip away and return to her dormitory unawares and be done with it. She took a few more steps back but stopped when she heard her name.

"...Miss Bell could join me on Sunday. I know it's a lot to ask, especially on the Sabbath, but I promised Jimmy, and I don't want to disappoint him."

Lieutenant Worthington wanted her to join him? For what? A church service? How odd.

Liam finally addressed her. "Miss Bell? Oh, there you are. Come into the light, miss. Lieutenant Worthington requires your help."

Addi rejoined the men, still smarting from the snub but battling a growing curiosity. "Help with what, sir?"

Lieutenant Worthington almost smiled. But not quite. "I promised my son that he could accompany me on a lighthouse visit. But I must inspect the light and property thoroughly, and it's too dangerous for Jimmy to climb about and follow me around. So I have requested that you accompany us to the Rock Island Lighthouse this Sunday." He addressed the darkness over her shoulder, as if afraid to look her in the eye now, and his somber tone stirred discomfort in her chest. "I know it's a day of rest, but for me, Sundays are rarely that. Besides, the keepers have a child, and they invited me to bring my son."

"Sir, your wish is our command. Naturally, Miss Bell will accompany you and your son." Liam chuckled, bowing to the lieutenant.

Addi blinked. Without even asking her? Without addressing her? Certainly, Liam was her superior. But he could at least allow her the dignity of agreeing to the expedition. Ire surged the blood in her veins, causing perspiration to prick her temples. She swiped it away as discreetly as she could with her fingertips.

The Navy man didn't acknowledge her, either, speaking only to Liam. "I will expect her at the docks at eight sharp. We will probably not be back until nightfall, so she should bring a cloak and a change of clothes in case she gets wet, as Rock Island is barely above water."

"Very good, sir. We aim to please." Liam nodded.

Lieutenant Worthington snapped an almost imperceptible glance her way, then turned back to Liam. "Good evening, sir."

When he had left, Addi huffed. "Are you quite serious? Am I invisible? Am I a slave?" As she fired the questions off, Liam's brow furrowed, but she wasn't done. "Yes, I am your employee. But I am a person, am I not? That whole time, you two talked *about* me without the decency of even addressing me."

His lips pursed into a frown. "I am *so* sorry, Addi. I often get so caught up in serving our clientele, well, I forget my manners. It's one of my worst faults—among many. Will you forgive me, please?"

So expeditiously repentant. So much like Papa. He was always quick to ask forgiveness after he'd been the least bit grouchy or short with her. A good virtue that would cover most any vice—so long as one did not keep repeating the infraction.

Her shoulders relaxed and her anger dissipated like a morning dew. "Oh, all right. But next time, please include me in a conversation that's about me."

Liam fidgeted, shifting from one foot to the other. "I...I am sorry, Miss Bell. I will do my best in the future."

Addi forced a smile. "Forgiven."

For several minutes, they stood in comfortable

silence enjoying the wonderful music they had come to hear. When the orchestra played "Three Little Maids from School are we" from Gilbert and Sullivan's *Mikado,* Liam pretended to wave a fan and made a silly, puckered-up face. Addi covered a giggle so she'd not draw attention to them.

Suddenly, she turned to Liam and whispered, "Goodness! It must be getting late. What time is it?"

Liam pulled out his pocket watch. "Half past nine."

Now it was her turn to fidget. "I missed curfew. Mrs. Erving will have my head on a platter."

"She can't fire you. You are my employee. Still, we'd best get you back and save that pretty neck of yours." He chuckled.

And save her reputation as well.

*L*iam paced the early morning dew-laden grounds of the island, trying to work off his frustration in the quiet of the mist. A passing ship sounded a warning in the rapidly thickening fog. Like a feral cat, the ground cloud swept in so silently, he'd barely noticed that he could scarcely see the pavilion just a hundred feet away. The heavy, pregnant drops of moisture wet his face and hands as the cold, gloomy quiet sent him scurrying for the building.

Just minutes earlier, Mrs. Erving had accosted him on his way to open the recreation center for the day.

The woman scowled and fairly growled her concern over Miss Bell, *his* employee, threatening to escalate her complaint to the hotel management. It took a bit of skillful excuse-making to smooth her ruffled feathers.

The nerve of Gert tattling like a schoolgirl about Addi's late arrival at the boardinghouse. And embellishing the tale, having her returning after midnight. He just knew the pudgy kitchen maid would be a thorn in Addi's side. Jealous, no doubt, of Miss Bell's amiable ways and beautiful countenance.

Aye, he'd also noticed Gert's interest in him. Batting her lashes over those bulgy eyes. Changing her tone when she addressed him to a syrupy sweetness that made his skin crawl. Leaning in when he spoke. Blathers! The thought of her made the oatmeal curdle in his stomach.

If only she wasn't Addi's roommate.

Should he inform Addi of the encounter or leave it be? After last night's vexation, his reticence to step into another confrontation with her so soon held him at bay. Why should it matter? She was his employee, after all. After entering the pavilion, he went straight to the reception desk to check the day's schedule.

"Good morning, sir. A rather dreary day, wouldn't you say?" Addi's warm smile dispelled the morning's gloom, at least inside the pavilion. "Will it clear?"

"The fog should burn off by mid-morning. It usually does."

Her eyes twinkled. "Good. Because I had planned to

take the children out to catch bugs and critters for our terrarium. Care to join us?"

A guffaw escaped his lips. The woman had a way of surprising him with her unconventional ways. He wiped away his mirth. "Sorry. The idea of a prim, proper, pretty young woman picking up worms and frogs and bugs tickles my funny bone."

She grinned, a shrug her only defense. "Guilty as charged, but I rather relish the opportunity to enlighten my children with a learning experience that they'll remember always. And thank you for the 'pretty' compliment."

Heat rose up his neck and burned his cheeks. He glanced around, but thankfully, none of the other employees—or patrons, for that matter—were about. Perhaps it had gotten him back into her good graces.

"Just stating the facts, ma'am. Thank you for the invitation. I'll try to get away from the desk if it's not too busy."

"Splendid. The boys, especially, will enjoy a male perspective on such an adventure. But now, if you'll excuse me, I must prepare for the day."

Hours later, after he'd dealt with a scuffle over who won a card game and minor leak in the men's shower, Addi emerged from her room with all six children in tow. Two carried pots with lids. Two carried nets. And two carried glass jars with holes in the lids. As they joined him at the desk, the children fairly danced their excitement.

The group quietly waited for him to finish giving directions to a man who wanted to join a card game. Then Addi grinned, a little mischievously. Adorable. "Are you free to go critter catching with us, Mr. Donovan?"

"Please? It'll be fun." Jimmy peeked around the desk.

Liam chuckled. "Well, when you ask me so nicely, young man, how can I resist?"

He turned the management of the pavilion over to his assistant, Mr. Tison, and joined the adventure.

He opened the door for the lot of them, gifting Addi with a wide smile. "I may know just the right spot for finding small frogs and perhaps even a turtle. Follow me."

Liam led them to the south end of the tiny island where he'd seen the little brown amphibians near a small rocky marsh. Sure enough, he scooped up one the size of a quarter and showed the children before plopping it in Nora's jar. "This is a spring peeper. You can tell because it has a cross on its back. See?" He pointed to it as the children *ooh*ed and *ahh*ed. "Moreover, they're called spring peepers because they make a loud, high-pitched, chirping sound, especially in the spring, and when a group of them sing together, it sounds like sleigh bells."

Addi nodded. "Thank you, Mr. Donovan. Now we need to find some bugs, like ants and beetles, for our little frog friend to eat."

"I don't want to see him eat bugs." Sally scrunched up her face and shook her head.

Addi touched her shoulder, bending down to comfort her. "But that's what they eat, just like we eat chicken."

The three boys had already found a small black-ant hill and were collecting them by the handful and putting them into Jimmy's pot. Markie plucked two fat worms from the ground and added them. The girls stood by, not at all interested in touching any of them.

Markie held a few ants in his cupped hands, ready to drop them in the frog jar. "Do we kill 'em first?"

"No need. The frog knows what to do." Addi held back a grin.

The child placed the ants in the jar, and quick as a wink, the frog thrust out his tongue and gobbled them up.

Nora nearly dropped the jar, but Addi steadied it—and her. "Ewww...that's gross."

Once the boys loaded the pot with handfuls of ants, Jimmy plopped on the lid.

Gregory pointed to the shoreline and yanked Sally's net from her hands. "There's some water beetles, but they're in the river."

Addi hurried to his side. "Gregory, hand that back to Sally and ask for it nicely, please."

"But the beetles might swim away."

"Hand it back, young man."

Gregory harrumphed and gave Sally the net. "Can I have the net so I can catch the beetles? Please?"

Sally smiled and handed it to the eager boy.

Liam grinned. What an excellent mother Addi would make. She knew just how to handle her young charges with wisdom and kindness.

What might it be like to parent with her?

Goodness! Where had that notion come from? He'd had dreams of a large family since he was a wee lad, but wasn't such thoughts a bit premature at the moment? His heart took to trotting, so he put his hand to his chest.

Only time would tell if his boyhood dreams would one day come true.

CHAPTER 7

The morning sunshine dappled the river, sparkling like diamonds on a dark-blue cloth while the small Navy steam launch chugged downriver toward Sisters Island Lighthouse. Addi had never been on a boat before. Never traveled on the St. Lawrence River before. Despite the quandary of Lieutenant Worthington's aloof demeanor, what a splendid adventure this day should be!

The boat captain pointed to a large island on their port side. "That be Grenadier Island."

A huge freighter came toward them, and Jimmy wriggled in his seat. "I'd like to sail on one of those when I get big, Papa. The ship is bigger than that whole island, and look at all the sailors."

His father put a firm hand on the boy's shoulder. "Settle down, son. Being a salty sailor is not for you. They are an uncouth and uncivilized lot. Better to be a

Navy man." He turned his son's attention to the lighthouse. "Look here. That island is Sisters Island, our destination. And now, I need to finish preparing for the inspection." He opened a folder he held and consulted the papers inside.

Addi grasped Jimmy's hand and pointed to Sisters Island. "The island is long and skinny like a ship. Can you imagine living there?"

The lieutenant glanced up. "Captain William Dodge and his family live there. They built the lighthouse in 1870 to mark a dangerous shoal on the Canadian side of the shipping channel. But after the light was commissioned, they moved the channel to the American side."

Jimmy cocked his head. "How can they move water?"

He smiled. Barely. "A channel is like the road a ship takes, but it must be substantial. They had to blast the bedrock to make it deep enough for the big ships." He tapped his top paper with the square nail of his index finger. "It says here that in 1870, forty-three crew members worked on a drilling barge and were drilling holes, placing dynamite in the channel, when lightning hit the barge."

Addi sucked in a breath. "Goodness! What a dangerous job."

Lieutenant Worthington shrugged. "Progress calls for risks." The man was a confusing mixture of rugged handsomeness and military aloofness. His dispassionate indifference set her nerves on edge. "Unfortunately, the explosion killed eleven of the crew."

Why would he speak of such a tragedy in front of Jimmy? She stepped closer to Lieutenant Worthington and whispered, "Perhaps we should spare a child the details."

"Don't be preposterous, miss. Children must be prepared to face the world girded with the armor of reality and brandishing a sword of wisdom."

Her spine straightened. "Yes, sir. But wisdom from God is the best course, I believe, and not the harsh details of this fallen world."

Lieutenant Worthington pursed his lips.

She took in a shaky breath and dared to continue. "The Bible says to put on the full armor of God, with the belt of truth, the breastplate of righteousness, and with your feet fitted with the gospel of peace. And we must put on the helmet of salvation, take up the shield of faith, and take up the sword of the Spirit, which is the word of God. That, sir, is how we should prepare children."

The lieutenant's jaw dropped open, but he quickly snapped it closed. Instead of speaking, he returned to reading his paper silently.

When they disembarked, Addi took Lieutenant Worthington's icy hand as she stepped onto Sisters Island. She had offended him, of that she was sure. But why? She'd only spoken the truth.

Captain Dodge, his wife, and his son, whom she

guessed to be ten or so, met them at the dock. "Welcome to Sisters Island. Lieutenant Worthington. And you must be Master Worthington. And whom might you be, miss?"

Addi curtsied. Hadn't Lieutenant Worthington informed them of her joining the expedition? "Miss Addison Bell, a teacher from Thousand Island House. I'm here to tend to Jimmy while the lieutenant makes his inspection."

Mrs. Dodge grinned and slipped her hand into the crook of Addi's arm as if they were old friends. In a pale-blue dress with a dark-blue apron, the tall, willowy woman exuded comfort and welcome. "I haven't seen a woman in weeks. I'm glad you've come."

Addi took a whiff of the air and smiled. "Your island smells of honeysuckle and sunshine."

Lieutenant Worthington harrumphed as they headed toward the lighthouse. "More like dead fish and seaweed. Shall we begin, Captain?"

Jimmy waved to the back of his father before casting a crooked smile at the Dodge boy. "I'm Jimmy. I like your island."

"I'm Billy." His eyes were the color of the river, just like his mother's. "Wanna fish?"

Mrs. Dodge stopped him, shaking a thin finger. "After lunch, young man. Let's show our guests around the island, and then you boys can play until it's time to eat."

"Awww...Ma."

Billy folded his arms and pouted but followed his mother as she led them to a cement breakwall. The boys skipped stones along the way.

"Sisters Island actually consists of three tiny islands connected by this breakwall. It runs parallel and just south of the international border between Canada and the US that's right there in the middle of the river. You could actually swim to Canada if you wanted to."

Addi raised an eyebrow. "I don't swim. Do you? How do you keep your son safe out here?"

Mrs. Dodge waved her hand. "I swim, and we've been here since he was in diapers. He knows the limits, the dangers, and the joys of island life."

"Isn't it lonely? Island life, I mean."

"Sometimes. Especially in the winter. We are required to spend the entire year maintaining the light, even though it is extinguished during the winter months when the St. Lawrence freezes over. A silly rule we hope will change."

Addi shivered at the thought of being here in the severe North Country winter. All alone. Isolated. Worse than she and Papa were on the farm.

"Are you chilled, dearie?" Mrs. Dodge placed a hand on her forearm.

"Just thinking how cold it can get here, 'tis all."

And wondering how she could endure such confinement.

"Below zero many a day, with the winds howling and snow gathering so high it'll block the door. Yes, it's not for the faint of heart. But when it's warm and sunny and the mighty ships pass by, oh, it's magical."

"I can see that." Addi nodded. But still, thank goodness it wasn't her fate.

Billy jumped in front of her, nearly tripping her up. The curly-headed boy was almost as tall as she, with buck teeth and a wide grin. He slapped his chest. "I'm gonna be the keeper when Pa gets too old."

"He's been saying that since he was knee high to a toad." Mrs. Dodge adjusted her kerchief that the wind had blown askew.

Jimmy slapped his chest—a little too hard, bringing on a cough. "I'm gonna be a Navy man like my Pa."

Billy grinned. "Then you can inspect the light when I'm the keeper. Let's race to the house."

The boys counted—"one, two, three"—and took off running toward the two-and-a-half story limestone house. Decorative trusses and brackets at the ends of its side-gabled roof and two inset gable dormers adorned the steeply pitched roof, while the light tower rose high from the center of the house. Heavy limestone lintels and sills decorated the lighthouse's many windows. It was a beauty to behold.

Mrs. Dodge led Addi toward the front door. "They built the lighthouse in 1870. It was supposed to be made of brick on account of the weather, but they used limestone from Kingston, Canada, instead. I like it better. More natural, if you ask me. Warm too."

Addi smiled. "It's lovely."

Mrs. Dodge flashed her a grin. "It's home, though a unique one. The tower has a fixed Fresnel white lens with an illuminating arc of three-hundred-and-sixty degrees. It shines forty-seven feet above the river and keeps many a ship from perishing in these dangerous waters."

"This part of the river is that dangerous? How so?" Alarm quickened her pulse.

Mrs. Dodge clucked her tongue. "Many ships have sunk or gone aground along the St. Lawrence River. There are many, many deadly shoals just under the surface. A shipper's gotta know the lay of the river, and it ain't an easy span to traverse. But now, we'd better prepare some luncheon for our men and boys, else they might become dangerous too."

She guffawed at her quip, and Addi joined her in a polite laugh. As brief as their acquaintance would be, no need to correct the woman on her assumption that Lieutenant Worthington was *her* man. Does she even want a man?

Liam flashed into her thoughts, and a warm bath of hope surged through her veins. What if?

---

*A*ddi noticed the Lieutenant's frustration the second he entered the kitchen for lunch. His face taut. His eyes narrowed, glaring at her. What had she done? Did a little Scripture rile him that much? Better soften the mood, and quick.

"How's the inspection going, sir?"

Lieutenant Worthington frowned, as if trying to understand her simple question. When he answered, his tone was flat. "Captain Dodge is most professional. We've inspected the island's breakwater, walkways, and shoreline."

Mrs. Dodge motioned for them to take their seats. After a quick prayer, they began to eat and converse most pleasantly. "Would you like some gravy, Lieutenant Worthington?"

The lieutenant blinked. "Yes. Thank you, ma'am. Delicious meal."

Jimmy touched his arm. "But you haven't eaten a thing, Papa. Can you cut my meat, please?"

Addi answered from the other side. "Allow me, young man." She cast them both a smile and proceeded to cut his chicken into impeccable little bite-sized pieces.

"Sir? Can you pass the peas, please?"

Billy stared at the lieutenant with hand outstretched. He handed the boy the bowl of peas. "Sorry, son. I'm a bit distracted, I suppose."

What was wrong with Jimmy's father? He seemed rattled, distracted, irritated.

Captain Dodge chuckled. He gave her a long, warm glance and then winked at Lieutenant Worthington. Surely the captain didn't think that she and the lieutenant... "You've been distracted all morning, Lieutenant. Best fill your belly with my wife's good cookin'. That'll fix anything that ails you." He patted his abundant middle and stood to refill his water glass, limping toward the sideboard where the pitcher sat.

Jimmy set down his fork. "Does your leg hurt, Captain?"

Captain Dodge nodded. "Broke my foot while serving in the Civil War. That's how I got my title, captain. But after that, before I became a keeper, I was a cabinetmaker, tax collector, and census enumerator. This here sideboard is one of my creations." He slid his hand along the ornately carved buffet.

Mrs. Dodge smiled. "And a treasure it is, dear. Now sit down and tell the lieutenant about the well."

He poured his water and sat. "Two years ago, they sunk a well straight through the granite. It now gives us pure, sweet water from almost twenty-six feet down."

Addi didn't understand. "But the river is all around. Can't you use that water?"

Mrs. Dodge answered. "We can, but there are lots of impurities on the surface from the ships and boats and even the fowl. The deep water is clean and pure."

"And cold." Billy took a gulp of his water.

Mrs. Dodge turned to Lieutenant Worthington. "Where are you from, sir? Tell us about yourself, please."

Lieutenant Worthington sighed, patting his mouth with his napkin. "Albany, ma'am. Went to Peekskill

Military Academy from the time I was eight. Both parents died while I was there, so I joined the Navy as soon as I could. Been stationed in Buffalo ever since."

Jimmy waved his fork in the air. "The school was built near a hanging tree where a British spy was died. Right, Papa? They found his bones there and everything."

"That's right, son. And our motto was 'stand firm as an oak.'"

Jimmy grinned. "An oak is strong. I wanna go there, but not until I'm bigger. Grandmama teaches me, but she says she's getting too old to bother."

Billy swallowed before speaking. "Ma teaches me good. I can read and do sums and am smart as a whip, she says."

Better to turn the conversation, and quick, before the two boys got into a competition. But before she could steer the discussion to another topic, Lieutenant Worthington did. "Captain, tell me more about the shadfly problem you noted in your reports."

Mrs. Dodge wrinkled her nose and groaned. "Nasty creatures. Show up every year, them fleshy insects do. Sometimes they cover the ground like an ugly snow."

"They're more than just ugly." Captain Dodge continued the explanation she'd hijacked. "Sometimes they block the oxygen intake to the light and extinguish the flame. That causes a dangerous gas leak in the tower, so I have to keep watch all day and night when those unwelcome varmints come to visit."

"Oh my. What a misery." Addi cringed at the thought. "I know of them too. They're smelly things, but they don't bite or sting. And thankfully, their season is only a few weeks."

Mrs. Dodge nodded. "But then there's the cleanup. Sometimes it takes all day to rid the island of their carcasses. But now, on to a better topic. How about some blueberry buckle?"

After dessert, Captain Dodge and Lieutenant Worthington continued the lighthouse inspection while she and Mrs. Dodge sat outside in Adirondack chairs. The boys waded in the water and played together quite nicely. Perhaps she really wasn't needed on this outing, but she was glad she came nonetheless.

Addi's chair faced the house and the shore where the boys played, a perfect perch for keeping a keen eye on Jimmy and seeing how the lieutenant inspected the lighthouse. He checked the foundation, roofs, gutters, porch, steps, chimneys, and site drainage. Then the men went inside, probably to inspect the interior, she mused. Though not an expert, from what she'd seen, the Dodges kept an impeccable home and property.

Finally, the men climbed up to the light and inspected it. Upon returning, Lieutenant Worthington almost cracked a smile. Could a person be any more unreadable? "Immaculate. Hardly a smudge or dead fly. The Fresnel lens's hundreds of pieces of cut glass surrounding the lamp bulb sparkles as if new. Well done, Captain! I haven't seen a Fresnel lens this clean in several years of inspecting. You've left me no choice but to give you an A-plus rating."

Captain Dodge grinned like a child with his first lollypop. "Thank you, sir. I pride myself on taking care of her. After all, she is often the difference between life and death, and I want no fatalities on my doorstep."

"Pleased to hear it. And now, let's go over your ledgers."

She and Mrs. Dodge chatted like old friends until the men returned to their side. "Shall we be on our way?" The lieutenant offered her his hand. She took it and stood, smoothing her skirts. After a round of good-byes, they stepped onto the launch to return to the Thousand Island House. Jimmy promptly fell asleep on the bench beside her while she told his father about him wading in the river, chasing frogs, playing checkers, and getting along splendidly with Billy.

He smiled. Actually smiled.

"That's the first time I've seen you smile, Lieutenant. It's nice to see."

He stared at her until she squirmed in her seat. "How would you like to see me smile more often?"

Her thoughts flashed confusion. The man was a conundrum. "Sir? I think we should all smile more often. It brings a little more joy to the world."

He cleared his throat and rubbed his palms on his pants. "Why don't you come back to Buffalo with Jimmy and me? I think that would make us all smile more."

She swallowed hard, and she blinked several times

trying to understand his words. "Sir? You want me to be Jimmy's nanny? But I have a job here at the Thousand Island House."

"Miss Bell. I'm not seeking a nanny. I'm asking you to be my wife."

CHAPTER 8

Rain pelted on the classroom window, unlikely to stop for most of the day. Addi had planned to take the children on a nature walk. Now...what to do with six rambunctious kids?

And, even worse, what to do about Lieutenant Worthington? She'd barely slept for fretting about the untimely, inappropriate, uncanny proposal. And now, she'd have to engage with him today—and every day—when he brought Jimmy to class.

Be his wife? Why, the man must be mad! He hardly knew her. They'd shared but a few words, and Lieutenant Worthington had proven nothing but irritatingly contrary when they had talked. He rarely smiled, and for pity's sake, he was the last man on earth she would ever consider a proper match.

The man was a stiff, starchy uniform—and little more.

Trouble was, she hadn't answered him. He struck her dumb, and now she would have to deal with him eventually. Instead of giving him a quick, flat *no*, she had turned her attention to Jimmy and the islands beyond the boat, avoiding the Navy man all the way back to Alexandria Bay. Once on dry land, she'd scurried to the safety of her lodging as fast as her feet could flee the awkward situation.

How could she navigate communication with Jimmy's father without hurting the boy? She adored little Jimmy and had no intention of causing pain to the tender child. Surely, he'd noticed the cold distance between his father and her on the way back to the hotel. Thankfully, he'd not inquired as to why. What would she say if he did? That proposal, on top of being totally inappropriate, was a grownup problem a child shouldn't have to bear.

She perused the shelves and sighed. Plenty of table games, and plenty more group games tucked away in her memory from her years of teaching would fill the rainy day. The challenge, as always, would be keeping them quiet and avoiding a scolding from the pavilion manager. In the weeks she'd been here, she'd received no less than six reprimands from Liam, and though he'd been kind and gentle, the corrections still stung.

Her one-room schoolhouse had been another matter. Hundreds of feet from the nearest neighbor, the children could run and play and make as much noise as they wanted. She never had to reprimand them. She never received a scolding either.

But Liam was so much more than her scolding boss. He was her friend. And maybe more. Her thoughts, more often than not, were filled with him.

A sharp rap on the door drew her attention. Too early for her children. Liam entered, his bright smile revealing straight white teeth. "Top of the morning to you, fair lass. Looks as though you'll be cooped up with your wee chickadees today."

Addi bobbed a quick curtsy, although she didn't really need to. They'd formed a bond, of sorts, she and her charming manager. The thought warmed her cheeks and stole her breath away. She swallowed before answering. "Yes, but there's plenty here to keep them occupied."

Liam scanned the shelves as he drew near. Then he touched her temple, as gentle as a summer's breeze. "And more in there, I reckon."

His touch sent a warm, pleasant rush to her heart, so unlike the cold touch of the lieutenant's hand. "True. I shan't be at a loss for things to do."

Liam folded his hands and drew in a jittery breath. As if he were nervous. Another scolding? Over what?

"How was your day with the Worthingtons? Did you fare well on your adventure to Sisters Islands?"

Gracious! How would she answer that? A tiny groan escaped her lips, and she licked them before pasting them shut. She couldn't besmirch a hotel patron, could she?

Liam must have noticed her angst, for his eyes flashed concern. "What's wrong, Addi? Your face betrays it might not have been altogether pleasant."

Just then, Sally and Markie burst through the door. Markie held something in his hand. "Look, Miss Addi. I found two slugs. Will the frog like them? Papa thinks so."

Whew! Saved by slimy slugs. "Good morning, children. Yes, I do believe the frog would enjoy the treat. Why don't you place them in the terrarium carefully?"

Markie wrinkled his nose in triumph. "I knew it. See, Sally. I knew Froggie would like them."

"Slugs are disgusting." Sally scrunched up her face.

Before Addi could respond to Liam, Lieutenant Worthington and Jimmy entered the room. The lieutenant didn't acknowledge her but held out his hand to Liam. "Good morning, Mr. Donovan. Stormy day out, eh?"

Liam glanced at her before responding. Something in his eyes begged a question she didn't want to answer. "True enough. I do hope it clears, though I'm not too sure it will."

The Navy man shrugged, training his eyes on Liam. "No matter. I have an extensive report to write about Sisters Island and the lighthouse. Good man, that Captain Dodge."

Liam nodded at Lieutenant Worthington, but cocked an ear as little Jimmy spoke to her.

"Morning, Miss Addi. I had fun with you yesterday, but Papa was really sad all night. And grouchy too..."

The tension between Jimmy's father and her was palpable. Surely, Liam felt it too.

She glanced at her employer, whose eyebrows rose at the declaration. Then she peeked at Lieutenant Worthington, whose face turned scarlet as his eyes narrowed to tiny slits.

"James Worthington. That is enough idle chatter, young man. Go and play with the children. Now!"

Tension would be an understatement.

Jimmy's lip quivered and his shoulders sagged. She cast his father her fiercest scowl and grasped Jimmy's hand, tugging him toward the shelves of toys. "Why don't you find something to play with, and I'll be with you in a moment?"

Leaving the boy with Sally and Markie, she returned to the doorway where Lieutenant Worthington stood, arms folded over his chest, stewing.

"You needn't be so harsh with him, sir. Now is not the time or place to air your grievances." She stewed too. Shame on him for taking out his frustrations on the child.

"Tonight, then, Miss Bell." Lieutenant Worthington harrumphed, his eyes cold and tone colder. Without waiting for a response, he marched out of the room and out of sight.

Addi blew out a breath. What would she say to Liam, who had witnessed the altercation?

Jimmy ran up to her and tugged on her skirt. "Don't worry, Miss Addi. Grandmama says Papa only speaks Navy. That he doesn't know how to be civil with people who aren't in the Navy, and that Papa and Mama were strangers in the night. What does that mean, Miss Addi?"

Addi bit her lip. Oh my. "You'll have to ask your grandmama, dear boy. That is beyond my expertise. Now go and play and don't worry about that little tiff."

Jimmy smiled and fled her side, leaving her with Liam's questioning gaze.

"I'll not ask the details of that strangely stress-filled confabulation, but I hope you can settle the situation before it brings any more angst into your classroom, Miss Bell."

Miss Bell? That was never a good sign. "Yes, sir. I'll take care of it before the day's out."

"I'm here, friend, if you need a listening ear." Liam touched her forearm gently.

Addi curtsied. "Thank you, Liam. I'll be fine."

But would she?

*L*iam loitered around the pavilion at close of day. Finally, Lieutenant Worthington entered the building, his military march and full-dress uniform exhibiting—no, demanding—attention. Power. Superiority.

Blathers! What did that man do to create the tension he had observed that morning? He had never seen the lovely lass so upset and nervous before. What happened yesterday to make Addi so tense and the Navy man sad and grouchy, as his son had declared? Surely, there'd been an altercation of great magnitude on the excursion to or from the island.

He waited for a long while before Lieutenant Worthington exited her classroom with his son in tow. His face was stony cold, and the boy's pout told him something went wrong.

Should he check on Addi or let her be?

Oh, the quandary of balancing his position as manager and his growing feelings for Miss Addison Bell. He had vowed to not become emotionally engaged with anyone after Tina had hurt him so.

But this was a staffing problem. Why shouldn't he make sure his *employee* was all right?

He sucked in a steadying breath before hurrying down the hallway and tapping on the door. Slowly, he entered the room to find Addi with her back to him, hovering over the terrarium. She didn't turn to greet him. Didn't acknowledge his presence.

Just as Lieutenant Worthington and he had done to her.

He cleared his throat to announce his presence. "Good evening, Miss Bell. How was your day?"

She swiped her face with her hands, and when she turned around, red rings betrayed that she'd been crying.

Alarmed, he hurried to her side. "Are you all right, miss? Did the lieutenant hurt you? Please be honest with me, for I will not allow anyone, patron or otherwise, to abuse my employees."

"Is that all I am?" Her brow furrowed as if she struggled to understand his words.

She sniffled, her shoulders sagging in defeat. She plunked down in a nearby chair and sighed, her face so sad, it nearly brought a tear to his eye.

Instead, his heart took to trotting. What should he say to that question? "No. Umm...yes. Umm...should I not care about my staff's well-being?"

She touched the terrarium, deflecting his question. "Thank you for the bowl. The frog is quite popular with the children. They love the terrarium." She pulled a pink embroidered handkerchief from her pocket and wiped her nose.

Did changing the subject mean she didn't want to talk about it? Should he press her to answer him?

He decided not.

"I'm glad the children are enjoying it, but I sense this has been a difficult day for you, Addi. I've experienced some bad days too. The worst was when my fiancé left me at the altar to marry my best friend. I thought my world had ended, but I found solace in focusing on my career. That tragic betrayal was for the best, though I couldn't see it at the time."

Her eyes brimmed with tears that spilled over onto her cheeks. He pulled his handkerchief from his pocket and gently dabbed them away.

"Tell me what's wrong. Please?"

The word *please* sounded as though he was whining, but he didn't care. Something was terribly wrong, and if that man had abused her, Liam would have his head on a platter, Navy or not.

For several moments, she said nothing, and it took all the self-restraint he had to not demand an answer. He waited. He prayed. Hopefully, she'd explain her situation and he'd be able to help.

Finally, she spoke, her voice quivering with emotion. "He asked me to move to Buffalo with them."

Incredulous! The man had the gall to steal his employee?

"But you already have a job. Can he not find a nanny for the boy in that large city?"

Addi bit her bottom lip and squared her shoulders. She took a breath and seemed to find strength from deep inside her. "Not to nanny. To be his wife!"

What? Who did he think he was? Lieutenant Worthington barely knew her. Not like he did. In his anger, he swallowed wrong, sending him into an embarrassing fit of coughing and choking for several long minutes. When he'd finally found his breath again, her pinched lips and shaking shoulders betrayed her holding back a spark of amusement.

"And you think it's funny to see me choking?"

"Goodness, no. It just appears that you think the lieutenant's proposal as ludicrous as I do."

Hope danced a jig in his chest. "Ludicrous? You're not going to marry him?"

"Of course not. He's an empty suit, void of any relational skills whatsoever. But I fear this situation may cause you trouble. He said he'd report me as a sub-standard employee of the Thousand Island House hotel and demand my dismissal. That is the reason for tears."

"Blathers! On what grounds? He'll not hog tie me with his demands, and he won't cause you any more pain, if I can prevent it. Chin up, dear one. I'll take care of this scrappy Navy man in two shakes of a lamb's tail."

A tiny tremble in her jaw caused no little consternation. Did she doubt him? Fear the lieutenant?

"I didn't mean to be a bother, sir. I was just trying to do my job as you wished. I had no idea he'd make such a declaration, nor did I encourage it. In fact, I gave the man a bit of a lecture when he'd been harsh with his boy, even quoting Scripture to him. He had no reason to think I might be interested in any kind of relationship except to care for Jimmy."

Liam shrugged. "Some men are as thick as a thousand-year bog. They go a bit muddled in the head when they see a pretty face and an opportunity to use a woman for their own purpose. Be assured, my lovely lass, that I will take care of this situation before the sun rises. Just you mind that."

At long last, he plucked a smile from her, although it didn't yet rise to her eyes. "Thank you, sir. Perhaps I shall be able to sleep tonight, after all."

"And now, to escort you home." He extended his elbow. Would she have the courage to take it? "We wouldn't want you accosted by a certain lieutenant, would we?"

She shook her head and took his arm. "Not tonight, nor any night, as far as I'm concerned. He was so angry with me when I refused his hand. How will I respond to him when he brings Jimmy to class?"

Liam pondered the predicament for several moments. "Hopefully, he won't stay here the entire summer. Until he departs, I will make sure that I am here when the children come and when they are picked up. And I will not offer your services to him again."

"Thank goodness for that. I appreciate your attentiveness, kind sir."

And I enjoy giving it. He'd protect her with his last breath, he would. Especially seeing her gaze at him with appreciation that he hoped would grow into affection.

CHAPTER 9

$\mathcal{A}$ddi scrawled one of her favorite sayings on the board in perfect Spencerian script. *Count your joys instead of your woes; count your friends instead of your foes—an Irish saying.*

She'd count her joys, all right—the most important was Liam being true to his word. He had skillfully smoothed over Lieutenant Worthington's ruffled feathers, and he'd kept the lieutenant from reporting her and demanding her dismissal. How he'd managed that, he wouldn't say, but she was grateful, nonetheless.

And for the past two weeks, Liam had even kept the Navy man under his strict scrutiny by faithfully being present when the nannies or parents dropped off their children and picked them up. Moreover, she didn't have to watch Jimmy past the ordinary class time.

But the icy interactions with Lieutenant

Worthington never warmed, never softened, even when Jimmy tried his best to get them to talk. The silent glares, the hardened jaw, the refusal to even answer a simple question about his son engendered unnecessary tension every day.

Yes, she counted Liam a friend, and their growing friendship dispelled the gloom of that strain day in and day out. But what would become of that relationship when the season was done and she didn't work at the Thousand Island House hotel anymore?

Gregory burst through the door with a kite in his hands. "I got a kite, Miss Addi. Can we fly it today?"

She glanced out the window. Sunshine, puffy clouds, and gently dancing leaves on the trees brought a smile and a nod. "I think that would be delightful, young man. If you'll share with the others."

"Awww...do I gotta?" The child stuck out his bottom lip in an exaggerated pout.

Addi touched the kite. "If you want to fly it, you must share, child. Not all the time, mind you. But sometimes. Now why don't you set it on that empty shelf before the others come?"

Gregory shrugged and did as she had bid, and two by two, the other four children entered with smiles and cheerful attitudes. She'd taught them to greet her and then each other first. After that, they were free to play quietly with the toys until everyone had come. All five did just that.

But where was Jimmy? And where was Liam?

For several minutes, Addi watched the door, hoping Liam would appear before Jimmy and Lieutenant Worthington did. She hadn't faced the man alone since that night, and she didn't want to today either. Perhaps Jimmy wasn't coming?

As with every day, Addi began the day with circle time. She'd gather the children around the board, talk about the quote, pray, and sing before any other activities. "All right, children. Put away your toys and gather in our circle, please."

She'd also taught them to clean up after themselves —well, most of the time. And truth was, she had Liam to thank for that too. She'd had one too many gentle scoldings from the man and had vowed to not have another.

Before the children had settled in the circle, Jimmy scampered into the room. "Sorry I'm late, Miss Addi. Papa had to talk to Mr. Liam."

He plunked down next to Markie, who had become the boy's shadow. Jimmy smiled at each of his friends and waved a greeting.

She grinned at the group of children, who had wiggled their sweet little selves straight into her heart. Each one so different—and so special. Even Gregory, who continued to be a bit of a bully at least once or twice a day. She prayed for them all—but for him the most.

"Let's listen to our quote for the day and talk about

it. *Count your joys instead of your woes; count your friends instead of your foes.* What do you think that means?"

Sally raised her hand. "It's how you look at life. Enjoy your friends and the happy things that happen, not the bad things."

The little girl had keen insight. "Very good. Other thoughts?"

Markie spoke next. "When Gregory is mean, I count him as a friend, anyway."

"Hey, watch what you say about me." Gregory scowled.

Addi had to put an end to this, and fast. "Friends may have troubles now and then, but they remain friends, right?"

The children nodded. Before she could continue, Jimmy shot his hand high in the air.

Addi bobbed her head, permitting him to speak.

"Is Papa your foe? Seems he gives you woes every day. Don't you like him, Miss Addi?"

The boy's eyes held no challenge, just innocent confusion.

But how was she to answer that, and in front of the entire class? "Your papa is not a foe, Jimmy. He is your father, and I respect him for raising you so well and for serving our country."

"But you aren't going to marry him?" Jimmy's brows furrowed.

The children gasped in unison.

Laura clapped her hands. "Really? You're getting married, Miss Addi?"

Gracious! How did this circle time get so off track? "No, I'm not getting married. It's time to pray."

Addi commanded them to fold their hands and close their eyes, but Jimmy's brimmed with tears and bewilderment. When he closed them, fat tears trickled down his face, and he swiped them away. She prayed. For their friendships. For their joys. For their day.

She turned to Gregory and swept her hand toward the shelf where the boy's kite dangled precariously on the edge. "Gregory has brought a special treat for us. Why don't you get it and show us?"

Gregory beamed, obviously pleased to be the center of attention. Like always. He jumped up and fetched his kite, quick as a jackrabbit, and returned to the circle. "I already told them about it, Miss Addi, but here it is."

He thrust it in the air. The single-line, silk-and-bamboo kite had a picture of an armor-clad knight brandishing a sword. A work of art, and obviously very costly. She'd have to ensure nothing happened to it.

She reached out and took the kite, silently bidding Gregory to sit with the others. "Mr. Benjamin Franklin was an inventor and discovered that lightning is natural electricity. Did you know Mr. Franklin and his son attached a key to their kite, flew it in a thunderstorm, and electrified it when lightning struck it? Don't ever try that on your own, though, for that is very dangerous."

Nora raised her hand. "Can we fly it today?"

Gregory answered with a nod. "And Teacher says I gotta let you try too."

Addi frowned, rubbing her chin. "But something is missing from this kite. Can anyone tell me what?"

The children stared, but none had an answer. She pretended to stroke an invisible tail, but that didn't give them a clue either. "What do dogs wag?"

"A tail. The kite doesn't have a tail!" Jimmy laughed, answering even before his hand rose.

Addi giggled. "That's right. Would you like us to make a tail for your kite, Gregory?"

The boy nodded, the children agreed, and they all set out to create the appendage.

And a very special memory, hopefully one that would lure Jimmy from his disappointment.

It was a good thing Liam's assistant manager relished the autonomy of taking the pavilion management so often, for that freed Liam to join Addi's kite-flying expedition. When she'd come to him for help, her anxiety over keeping the expensive toy secure had been evident. But he hadn't needed any arm-twisting.

He was happy to come to her rescue. But he hated the thought of having to deliver the news he'd been given earlier.

Later. He'd deliver it much later.

This was more important.

Not only did he enjoy being with Addi and the children, but the event also resurrected many wonderful memories of flying a kite he and his father made when he was a boy. Why had he never procured a kite for himself and flown it as an adult? For the joy it had brought him, he'd need to get crackin' and rectify that... and perhaps take Addi kite-flying again on her day off.

He followed her and the chattering children over the bridge to a high, grassy knoll next to the hotel. Then he pointed to the long pink ribbon he'd seen on Addi's straw hat—that was now bare. Small, colorful drawings twisted into makeshift bows completed the tail. "Children, this kite tail is a work of art! Did you make it?"

Each of the children showed him their drawings and explained their creations. Nora drew a rainbow. Laura, a bunny rabbit. Sally sketched several hearts, and Markie explained that his was a fish, though Liam was at a loss to guess what kind. Jimmy drew a bunch of stars, and Gregory said his drawing was a dragon that the knight had slain.

Liam sidled up to Addi and whispered in her ear. "That was kind of you, lass, to give up your hat ribbon for the cause."

"All in a day's work." Addi shrugged.

What creativity and ingenuity! "Aye, I've never seen the like of this tail. Your art makes this lovely kite a one-of-a-kind masterpiece. Well done, all."

She smiled, her eyes shining in the sunlight. "Has anyone flown a kite before?"

All the children shook their heads. Addi looked at him, and he playfully raised his hand, like a shy laddie reticent to answer. "My father and I made a kite and spent lots of days flying it in Ireland, but that was many a year ago. I'd be happy to show you how it's done. If I remember."

Nora grinned. "I'm sure you will, Mr. Liam. My family's Irish too. Gram and Gramps came from Dublin."

"I sailed out of Dublin when I was twelve, and I have been here ever since." He patted her head.

Addi smiled. "Well, children, do you know what's the most important thing you need to fly a kite?"

Several murmured, "A kite?"

Addi shook her head, waving her arm high in the air. "Wind. A kite won't fly without the wind. But the breeze can't be too strong or too weak. It has to be just right."

"Like Goldilocks's porridge?" Markie laughed.

Addi joined him with her giggle. He loved that sound. Like tinkling bells. "That's right. With a just-right breeze, a kite can soar and dance in the air. I've observed the fetching sight but haven't flown one myself."

Liam wagged his finger at the children, pasting on his strictest scowl. "But never, ever, ever fly a kite in a thunderstorm. It's very dangerous. And you don't want to be near trees, because trees eat kites."

Laura touched the kite. "Miss Addi told us about Benjamin Franklin."

He raised an eyebrow as he glanced in Addi's direction. "Aye, he was a famous inventor. Now, Gregory, it's your kite, so you can be the first flier, and I'll be the launcher."

Gregory stepped up and held the kite aloft, but Liam stopped him. "First, we need to decide which way the wind is blowing. The launcher—me—needs to have his back to the wind and face the kite into the wind. Otherwise, it'll crash to the ground. And you never launch it while running."

Several of the children nodded soberly. Six—no, seven—eager faces followed his every move. Addi's eyes twinkled with excitement too. He couldn't wait for her to have a turn.

Liam focused on Gregory. "As the flier, pay attention to the wind as well. Give the string a gentle tug now, and keep the tension on it so the kite will stay in the air. I will adjust my body so the wind is always at my back to show you the direction the wind is blowing. You line up with me, okay?"

"Okay. Ready!" Gregory fidgeted shifting from one foot to the other.

He faced the kite into the wind and instructed Gregory to take ten giant steps away, extending string but keeping it taut. When Gregory stopped, Liam waited for a gust of wind and released the kite. "Give it a tug, Gregory!"

Up, up, up the kite went, to the squeals and cheers of the children—and Addi. How endearing, the way she embraced life so much like a child, yet still with the grace of a lovely, accomplished woman. His heart skipped several beats at the thought.

The children waited their turns to fly the kite and be the launcher. Liam guided them, marveling at their patience and how they cheered each other on.

Finally, it was Addi's turn, but she tried to decline. "I don't need to, sir. The children must be tired."

"You gotta try it, Miss Addi. It's really fun." Gregory handed her the kite.

The children started chanting, clapping their hands in encouragement. "Teacher. Teacher. Teacher."

Addi took the kite and string, and her little ones cheered with glee. Following his guidance impeccably, she flew the kite high in the air, her face beaming like an angel's. Oh that he could see that face every day for the rest of his life!

But after he gave her the news, he'd see a much different face, he was sure. Better to let her know sooner rather than later.

Once everyone had flown the kite—and Gregory twice since it was his—they headed back to the pavilion. Lunch would be waiting, and she'd have the afternoon to adjust to the news.

As they crossed the river, Liam stepped up his pace to match Addi's. "I need to tell you something."

A gust of wind blew, and she caught her hat from flying away. "That was simply marvelous, *Mr. Donovan*. You're a very good teacher."

She glanced at Nora, who walked within earshot. She called him by his surname only when a child was near.

"Thanks. It was fun." Liam smiled, then lowered his tone. "Now, to the news. Did Jimmy tell you why he was late to class?"

"No. Is everything all right?" Addi's brows furrowed.

Liam nodded. "Yes. And no. Lieutenant Worthington paid me a visit this morning. He's returning to Buffalo soon, but he must inspect Tibbetts Lighthouse in Cape Vincent on Wednesday. As you know, it's a far distance from here, and he likely won't be back until very late, so he needs you to watch his son until he returns."

She stopped in her tracks and shoved her fists on her hips. "But that's tomorrow. And you said you'd not make me do that. Oh, Liam, I cannot. I will not!"

Heat rushed to his face, warming it as though he stood near a bonfire. He glared at her. *Won't? How dare she? Blathers!* She was an employee of the hotel, and it was their responsibility to serve the hotel patrons and meet their needs.

He calmed himself to a slow boil, measuring his words—and tone—carefully. "I'm sorry, but there is no one else he trusts with his child. I know it's a rotten bit of luck, but it'll be the last time, and he'll be gone by the weekend. Please? It's only this one time, and we are obligated to serve our patrons, Miss Bell."

Addi's students had continued walking toward the pavilion without her. Her eyes darted from them to him and back again, her face hard. Cold. "Do it yourself."

She took off running, leaving him standing there with his breath stolen by her ire.

CHAPTER 10

The early-morning sunshine burst through her classroom window, warming her face. Addi closed her eyes, taking in the warmth. She needed its life-giving strength to face the day ahead.

When the door opened and Liam entered, she whipped around, arms folded.

"Oh, all right. I'll do it. But only here in my classroom."

She bit her bottom lip, waiting for Liam to agree to her compromise. She'd tossed and turned the night away, fuming that he'd put her in such a position. She wouldn't go to the lieutenant's suite, no matter what. She'd make a pallet for the boy to sleep on right here in her room. Professional. Safe.

"Furthermore, you must be around the pavilion and safeguard me until Lieutenant Worthington picks up his son. No matter how late it is."

"Aye. I wouldn't have it any other way. Thank you, Addi. I'm sorry to put this on you after all that's transpired." Liam touched her shoulder.

Addi sighed and unfolded her arms. "As long as you're here, it'll be fine. But we'll also need an evening meal."

"As will I. I'll let the kitchen know." Liam grinned. He opened his hand, presenting her with a brand new pink ribbon. A peace offering of sorts.

"Thank you. I must admit, my hat looks rather forelorn without it."

Hours later, Addi had broken up two fights that Gregory had started. The child had entered the room in a foul mood, and no matter what she did, he wouldn't shake it. He smacked Markie when he won at checkers. He tripped Jimmy for no apparent reason.

"One more incident, young man, and I'll send you back to your nanny."

Gregory didn't budge. He balled his fists and stood his ground. "I don't care. I don't wanna be here, anyway, with all these babies. I'd rather be with Nanny."

She put a gentle hand on his shoulder. "But you'll miss our nature walk. Froggie needs some fresh bugs."

Gregory shrugged and said nothing. Then he reached over and pinched Laura, making her cry.

"That's it! You cannot be here today. You children behave while I'm gone. I'll be right back." She grabbed hold of his hand and tugged him toward the door.

After delivering Gregory to Liam to be sent back to his

nanny, she returned to a quiet and peaceful classroom. As she'd done daily, she read a story to the children. Today, she continued to read *The Five Little Peppers and How They Grew.* For days now, the children had enjoyed hearing how the Peppers lived, learned, and played in their little brown house. And how, though they were poor and their mamsie had to work constantly, their lives were happy.

But in today's chapter, the youngest, Phronsie, was kidnapped by an organ grinder, and the children gasped and wiggled nervously. Perhaps she should stop the story? No, the rescue, she knew, was just ahead.

"Don't fret, wee ones. It'll be okay. Let's hear how it all turns out for good."

Wide eyes stared at her. Expectant little bodies leaned forward.

Sure enough, Phronsie was rescued by a boy named Jasper King and his dog, Prince, and they all became friends. Then Jasper and his father invited the Peppers to visit their home in the city, and soon the entire family was living there.

Gert entered the room with their meal, a scowl on her face, as usual. Why couldn't the woman be pleasant for once? Even sharing a room was nothing short of disagreeable.

Addi snapped the book shut. "We'll continue the rest of the story another day. Now let's have lunch, and then we'll take our nature walk."

Gert set down the tray, gawking at the class. She

harrumphed. "A child is missing. Another ration of food gone to waste."

Addi shrugged. "He just left, Gert. The children will share the extra sandwich and carrots. Thank you for bringing them."

Suddenly, the door swung open, and a woman walked in dragging Gregory by the hand. "What's the meaning of this? Banishing my poor son from his class-room? How dare you?"

Gert grinned, and Addi stood and smoothed her skirts. "Thank you, Gert. You may go."

The kitchen maid left as Addi gathered her wits. The buxom woman's face was red as a beet. She wore fine clothes and a hat with a peacock feather sticking high in the air. It had to be Mrs. Hughes, Gregory's mother. She'd only ever seen his nanny.

"I'm sorry, missus. Gregory smacked a child, tripped another, and pinched a third. I cannot allow it in my class."

Mrs. Hughes harrumphed. Gregory looked up at his mother with eyes as innocent as a newborn babe's. He shook his head in protest.

"I had to leave my garden tea party to deal with this, miss. My nanny left last night. Ran off with some local rapscallion and left me with no child care. I can bring my baby to the party, but not him."

So that's why Gregory was so upset. She bent down and looked him in the eyes. "I'm so sorry you've lost your nanny. Will you promise to be kind to the children and obedient to me?"

"Yes, Miss Addi. I'm sorry." Gregory's eyes brimmed with tears.

She smiled and took his hand. "Well then, you're just in time for lunch and our nature walk."

"In future, miss, know my son does nothing wrong unless he's provoked. Just you mind that." Mrs. Hughes sighed.

Addi opened her mouth to argue but thought better of it. "I'll take good care of him, ma'am."

The woman left, and she closed the door gently behind her. Another crisis averted. For now.

When they had finished lunch, true to her word, Addi took the children on a nature walk. They crossed the bridge to the mainland, walking along the shoreline to the northeast. Markie found three black bugs, and with a stick, Gregory dug up two worms. The girls gathered shells and put them in their pockets until they brimmed over. Jimmy ferreted out a small garter snake and chased the girls around with it until Addi had to scold him.

"The Bible says that foolishness is bound in the heart of a child, Jimmy. That was foolish. Apologize, please."

Jimmy's heart might be foolish at times, but it was tender, and he did as she bid. As usual. Though he often did silly things, she'd never seen him rebellious or outright disobedient. If only his father could be handled as easily.

"I'm sorry, girls. Truly."

She patted him on the back. "Let the snake go, please, way over there in the tall grass."

On their way back to the pavilion, they ran into Mel and his group of big kids. Several of the children greeted one another.

Addi followed their lead. "Good afternoon, Mel. What are you up to today?"

Mel slapped the rolled-up newspaper he held. "We were just getting ready to play Fox and Hounds. Wanna join us?"

"Why not? If the children want to." She drew her children close. "Would you like to play Fox and Hounds with these kids?"

Her class cheered, except for Jimmy. He pouted, so she whispered, "What's wrong?"

"I don't know how to play," Jimmy whispered back.

"Oh, it's easy. One child is the 'fox.' He's given an old newspaper and drops a few small pieces of paper to make a trail. Then he runs and hides from the other children—who are the hounds. The hounds track him down and catch him. It's lots of fun."

Jimmy shrugged. "Okay, as long as I don't have to be the fox."

"I'll make sure of that." She took his hand and squeezed it.

The child had so little understanding of play and groups and relationships. No wonder. His father kept him isolated and alone most of the time. Perhaps her undivided time with the child tonight could help the sweet boy see what a treasure he is?

Brimming with anticipation, Liam tapped on Addi's classroom door and then let himself in. Even babysitting Jimmy Worthington would prove a pleasure with her. He'd known she'd rise to the occasion as soon as she had a chance to consider it. Why, she even handled the livid Mrs. Hughes and the ornery Mel with kid gloves.

He smiled at the sight of Addi and the wee lad playing checkers. "So we're having a special get-together, just the three of us, aye?"

Jimmy's eyes lit up when he saw him. "Yes, Mr. Liam. Papa's inspecting a lighthouse far away. I gotta sleep here until he comes."

"That's right, son. But until then, let's have some fun. What do you have planned, Miss Addi?" He cast her a quick wink.

Jimmy burst out before she could answer. "Can we go fishin'? I've asked and asked Papa, but he never has time."

He shook his head. "Sorry, Jimmy. It's too windy for fishing. Another time, perhaps."

"But I'm leaving in three days." The child stomped

his foot to punctuate his disappointment. "I'll never get to fish."

Addi took Jimmy's hand and led him to the shelves. "How about dominoes, tiddlywinks, pickup sticks, or jacks?"

"Okay, Miss Addi." Despite his agreement, Jimmy's pout remained unaltered, his eyes sad.

"Have you played before?" Liam pulled the dominoes off the shelf and began setting up the game while Addi put away the checkers.

Jimmy shrugged. "Not really. I've built with them, but not played a game."

Addi smiled. "No problem. Let's play Draw.' We'll put the tiles in the middle of the table, face down. Each player draws three tiles and looks at them. We leave the rest of the dominoes face down in the 'bone yard.' Whoever has the doublet with the most dots puts it on the table."

Jimmy's brows furrowed. "What's a doublet?"

"A domino with identical numbers on top and bottom, and doublets are put down sideways."

Liam continued her explanation. "The second player puts a domino with a matching number of dots against the doublet. The next player must lay a match at the free end of a tile. If he or she cannot, the player must choose new dominoes until he or she finds a match. The first player to lay down all of his or her dominoes wins."

The three of them enjoyed a rambunctious game

while talking about their favorite things—Addi's idea. He learned that her favorite color was blue. Her favorite animal was a *small* dog. Her favorite flower, a daisy. She thought them happy.

Before they finished the game, Gert came, bringing their meal. Liam jumped up and met her at the door. He took the tray, set it on a nearby table, and spoke in a quiet voice. "Thanks for doing this."

Gert harrumphed. "This is above and beyond my duty, sir. I've got plenty of work to do besides running hither and yon serving the likes of *her*."

"That's enough, miss. We serve at the pleasure of our guests, and this is for our guest, Lieutenant Worthington. If you have a problem, you can address him."

Gert groaned before lowering her voice and almost whispering to him. "Perhaps I will. And you'd better watch that one. I have evidence that there's much more to this than you think. The lieutenant has been giving her gifts. Maybe more than gifts, if you know what I mean." She slipped a locket into his hand. "Better not show her just yet. Make inquiries into her mischief and the giver of such an extravagant gift."

Heat rose from his chest to his cheeks, and small beads of sweat moistened his brow. "Watch your tongue, miss. I shan't have rumors and innuendoes fly about my staff."

The smirk on Gert's face should've given him pause,

but a twinge of jealousy took over, clouding his thoughts.

She tilted her head, tapping his hand. "I see how she comes and goes all hours of the night, and this is proof of such. Found it myself this morning."

He took a step toward Gert, causing her to back out into the hallway. "Thank you for dinner. As far as the rest of it, if you're slandering her, you'll be sorry."

Gert let out a huff and stomped down the hallway. He glanced at the silver locket in his hand. Shiny. New. It couldn't be a family heirloom. Could Addi truly have accepted such a costly gift from the lieutenant?

He opened the locket, but it was void of any picture. Or clues about the giver. He closed the front and shoved the jewelry into his pocket. He'd have to think about that later. And possibly do some sleuthing.

He entered the room to find that Addi had set their meal out in fine style. Chicken and dumplings and apple cake. Tall glasses of milk. Though he'd rather have tea or coffee, milk would do.

He prayed for the meal, and Jimmy ate with gusto. Liam smiled at him. "After we eat, I have a surprise for you."

"What is it, Mr. Liam?"

Addi wiped the boy's face and gently corrected him. "Please don't talk with your mouth full."

"After dinner," Liam promised him. When they'd finished the meal, he presented his surprise. "How would you like to go bowling? I reserved a lane, just for us."

"I don't know how." Jimmy hung his head.

"Neither do I, but we can learn together." Addi patted his hand.

The child lit up like a Christmas tree. "Okay, Miss Addi. Let's learn together."

And learn they did. Jimmy caught on quickly, but Addi struggled to make the ball go straight. He tried to help, but no matter what he said, it still went into the gutter. Finally, he wrapped his body around hers and guided her hand to release it with a smooth forward motion. A bold move, but no one else was in the bowling alley, save Jimmy.

Strike! Addi jumped up and down and wrapped her arms around him. But just as quickly, her eyes lit with awareness, and she plunged her hands into her pockets. Her face grew as crimson as a rose. "I'm sorry. I lost my head."

He leaned into her. "And a pretty head it is. No problem. Well done!"

When they returned to the classroom, the lieutenant was already there, pacing the floor. "Where have you been? I've been waiting for a half an hour."

"You're back early, Papa. We just went bowling, and I got a good score." Jimmy ran to his father and hugged him.

Lieutenant Worthington stayed stoic. Angry, even. "Yes, I finished early. You should have been here, son."

Liam stepped up. "My fault, sir. I reserved the alley and taught him to bowl. He's very good, sir."

"Very well."

The Navy man, dressed in his uniform as pristine as ever, touched his hat with two fingers. He stared at Addi for several seconds, the kind of stare that would make any woman nervous, before taking his son's hand and leaving.

No thank you. No appreciation. Nothing. The man was insufferable.

Suppressing a sigh, Liam offered his arm to Addi. "Shall I walk you home?"

Addi nodded. "That would be lovely. Thank you for being here. The man sets my teeth on edge. Never a smile or a thank you."

"But he likes you. Are you sure you've no feelings for him?"

Her brows furrowed and lips pursed before she answered. "I do not, sir."

He took her hand and slipped it into the crook of his arm. "Very good. Shall we?"

For now, he'd take her word for it. Later, he'd rule out Gert's ridiculous accusation. And then? Well, they'd just have to see what the future held.

CHAPTER 11

An hour later, Addi sucked in a steadying breath, but it didn't help. Her skin prickled and her heart took to trotting as she slammed her bedroom door and switched on the light. "Who do you think you are, stealing my locket and falsely accusing me? What have I ever done to you, Gert?"

The pain. The betrayal seeped through and into her tone.

Gert groaned, rolled over, and yanked the pillow over her head.

Oh no, she doesn't. She'll not bury her head and evade wrongdoing this time.

She stomped over to Gert's bed and tugged the pillow from her, forcing a much-needed confrontation. "You'll not ignore me on this one, miss. What gives you the right to cause such trouble for no reason?"

Gert kept her back to Addi, so Addi pulled off her covers. "Answer me, now!"

Like a lion ready to pounce, Gert rose out of bed, almost knocking her back on her heels, her buxom, chunky figure towering over her. Eyes darkened with challenge. "What gives you the right to be so high and mighty? I've done nothing wrong. You're always leaving things around my room. I found that trinket on the floor. Besides, the necklace is too new to be a family heirloom, so it's easy to guess where it came from. And you, flitting around with those men as though you owned the world. Scandalous!"

"Lies! All lies. I'd safely tucked that locket under my clothes in my drawer. You took it! And as far as who gave it to me, my father did before he died. Not that it's any of your business."

Gert shrugged, plunking herself down on the bed. A smirk twisted her fat cheeks. "An honest mistake."

Addi's breath caught in her throat and lodged there. Incredible! Quivering fingers flew to her face. No! She'd not lose this battle, no matter what. She balled her fists and straightened her shoulders.

With all the inner strength she could command, she lowered her voice and forced it to be strong and steady. "Gert, you know that's not true. You chose to take my locket out of my drawer. You chose to give it to Mr. Donovan and insinuate Lieutenant Worthington gave it to me. You chose to tattle to Mrs. Erving and suggest I was being inappropriate. You chose to lie!"

The kitchen maid stared at her for what seemed like hours, her menacing glare seemingly unaffected by the speech. She reached for her pillow, rolled onto her bed, pulled the covers over herself, and mumbled, "You've no way to prove any of that, so as far as I'm concerned, you're guilty of all of it unless you're proven innocent."

Suddenly, Mrs. Erving opened the door wide and stepped into the room. "I've had enough of this, you two. You'll wake the entire household with this loud prattle-prattle. Addi, get your things and come with me at once."

The woman's demand sent her body to tremble and her stomach to do flip-flops. She swallowed the bile that rose. "Yes, ma'am."

Mrs. Erving stood in the doorway, arms folded, until Addi had quickly shoved all her belongings into her worn carpet bag. Gert didn't move a muscle. Silently, Addi followed Mrs. Erving into the hallway.

The woman closed the door, touched her arm, and spoke gently. "Come with me."

What was going on? From anger to kindness in an instant? It didn't make sense.

The woman led her to the end of the hallway and opened the door. She switched on the light, bid her to enter, and closed them both inside. The room had one bed, a small table, a washstand, and a window. Was she to be locked in here until the authorities came to convict her? Her insides trembled as if it was ten below zero.

Mrs. Erving smiled and gently touched her cheek. "Take heart, Addi Bell. I had a visit from Mr. Donovan *and* the lieutenant a little while ago. As I suspected, Gert concocted these insinuations, accusations, and deceptions to disparage your name and have you dismissed. You needn't live under such persecution any longer, miss, so this will be your private abode for the rest of the season. *We* know the truth. But...we still have a problem."

She set her bag on the bed and swallowed her fears, but it didn't settle the turmoil she'd just endured. Vindicated? Just like that? And by Lieutenant Worthington, of all people? Her mind tried to grasp the twists and turns of the last several minutes.

"A problem?"

Mrs. Erving sighed. "Gert is the chef's favorite niece, and he's completely blind to her faults. She can do no wrong, and he will raise holy terror if we accuse her of anything. Can you bear it to forgive, forget, and move on without receiving the proper justice?"

"But that's so unfair." Her heart sank, and so did her shoulders.

"It is, but we've only a few more weeks, then the hotel will close for the season. Do we want the last days of our time here to be a battle? You know how Gert is, and I know how her uncle is."

Addi's head buzzed like a million bees had taken up residence. She couldn't think. And she was tired, so tired. "Can I answer you in the morning, please?"

"Of course. Get some sleep and pray about it. I know it's a lot to ask of you, since you've been so unfairly treated and falsely accused."

Her fight was gone. But her sense of right and wrong stayed solidly intact. "Thank you, missus. And thank you for this room."

"I should've moved you weeks ago, and I'm sorry I put you in with her in the first place." Mrs. Erving harrumphed.

Addi forced a smile. "You couldn't know this would happen. Good night, missus."

"I had an inkling. Shoulda followed it. Goodnight." Mrs. Erving's eyes flashed regret.

When the woman left, Addi plopped down on the bed. "Well, what do you know about that? Thank you, Lord."

She slipped onto her knees and thanked Him properly. For vindication if not for atonement. For Mrs. Erving and this room. For Liam coming to her aid yet again. Even for Lieutenant Worthington speaking the truth. And while she prayed, her heart fluttered to a place of peace. And forgiveness.

But how could she allow injustice to go unpunished?

That was another matter.

The next morning, Liam sat in his tiny, windowless office, stumped. He had no idea what to say to Addi. He'd never seen her so angry and confused as she blurted out the altercation with Gert and Mrs. Erving's response. Aye, the lovely lass had a bit of a temper. Best to keep that in mind.

Yet the inequity of allowing Gert to go free was contemptible. Disgraceful. Shameful. But Mrs. Erving had a point. He, too, steered clear of Chef's propensity to favor his niece—or anyone he took a shine to.

And it reminded him—too much—of how Tina had treated him, accusing him of things that never happened so she could justify her wandering affections and, ultimately, her marriage to another. It had been unconscionable and unforgivable. Yet, somehow, he'd forgiven her. Eventually. It cost him his friendship with several couples and, worst of all, his best friend. Neighbors, friends, and family believed the rumors Tina had spread. And no one knew the real story. She'd told tales that were untrue. Just like Gert had.

No, the choice to allow the guilty to go unpunished was no simple task, and only Addi could walk that road of sorrow. Like Jesus. He was falsely accused. Charged. Held accountable for others' wrongs. And He chose to not demand justice. Even more, He took the punishment!

He prayed for Addi. For the strength to choose. And

if she did make that life-altering decision, he'd...*know* how the rest of his life should go.

A rap on the door pulled him from his prayer. Addi stood in the doorway, eyes red, mouth downcast, shoulders slumped. As if she'd lost a great, awful battle. Perhaps she had.

Her voice quivered when she spoke. "Liam, would you have a few minutes to sit with my class so I can take some time alone to think? Please? I'm afraid I might snap at one of my darlings if I don't, and I can't bear to hurt one of those children."

Her deep brown eyes brimmed with tears, and her jaw quivered as if she might burst into sobs at any moment.

"Aye, of course, Addi. I can spare an hour, but then I have a meeting. Will that work?"

Her face relaxed a bit, but the sorrow and pain still stained her expression. "Thank you, sir. I shall return well before then."

What to do with six little children for an hour? Joining her class—with Addi in charge—was one thing, but being in charge of it and alone with six little ones shook him to the core. Easier to manage dozens of employees and organize the entire pavilion.

But he'd do it. For her.

He squared his shoulders and hurried to the room. In twos, the children happily and quietly played board games.

When Markie noticed him, he waved. "Hello, Mr. Liam. I'm winning at checkers. Come and see."

He greeted each of the children before joining Markie and Nora. "Hmmm...it looks like a close match. Are you having fun, Nora?"

"He's teaching me. I like to learn." The sweet little girl smiled.

"Good for you. And well done, Markie, in teaching her. I like to learn too."

Nora's brow furrowed, and a slight pout crossed her lips. "What's wrong with Miss Addi?"

Six pairs of eyes drilled Liam for an answer. The silence in the room was deafening. How could he answer that without revealing the true reason?

"Have you ever had a bad day and just needed time to sort everything out? I sure have."

Heads bobbed, but their faces sought more.

"Miss Addi just needs to think some things through. She's been faithfully taking care of you, so we can give her that much, can't we? What do you say to going outside and getting some exercise? A game of tag?"

The children cheered and ran to the door, question averted, at least for the moment.

He led the children to their favorite grassy spot on the island and engaged them in a rowdy game of tag, thankful no patrons milled about just then. He wanted to stay close, to keep an eye out for Addi, to be there if she needed him. Once the children were sufficiently winded and happy, they returned to the classroom to take up where they'd left off playing their board games.

"Welcome back, children. Mr. Donovan."

Addi had returned, her face washed and refreshed, a gentle smile lighting up her countenance. That was the best forty-five minutes he'd spent in a long time. What had happened for her?

He couldn't wait to find out.

When the last of her children left for the night, Addi tidied her classroom, erased the board, and checked on Froggie. He'd become an important part of the children's lives, and it would be sad to let him go when the summer ended. Hopefully, he'd fend well in the big, wide world out there.

"How was the rest of your day, Addi?"

She spun around and gasped, slapping her chest. "You scared me, Liam. I didn't hear you enter."

"Sorry. The door was ajar. I should have knocked."

"It's okay. I'm so much better after my brief respite. Thank you. And the children enjoyed the game of tag. They were pleasantly tired the rest of the day."

He bowed dramatically. When he straightened, the twinkle in his eyes and smile on his face set her heart fluttering like a butterfly. "At your service, my lady. Want to talk about your respite?"

She paused, gathering her thoughts. She'd tell him

everything, even revealing the weakness she'd rather hide.

"I do. As you well know, I have struggled to forego seeking punishment for Gert. I wanted retribution. But then, I remembered my papa quoting the book of Romans where Paul says, 'Avenge not yourselves... Vengeance is mine; I will repay, saith the Lord.'"

"My grandmother reminded me of that verse often." He chuckled, rubbing his chin as he often did when a little chagrinned.

She nodded. "Papa said I have an overactive sense of justice and made me memorize that verse. As a child, when something wasn't fair, I'd fuss and fume until I got into trouble, and I still struggle with this shortcoming. So this outrage with Gert hit me at the very core of injustice. Yet I am choosing to bow my knee and let God alone deal with it."

Liam took both of her hands in his and kissed them, and warmth like a sunny morning filled her being. When he spoke, his voice was husky with emotion. "I've been praying for you, Addi, to find peace in all this. Thank the good Lord, He answered my prayers."

"Thank *you*. Choosing to let God be God is hard, but it's the right thing."

"Always. And now, I have news for you."

He didn't let go of her hands. Instead, he gave them a gentle squeeze and pulled them a little closer to him. His eyes lit up, and a grin crinkled his cheeks. Oh, but he was a handsome man!

"Good news, I hope?" Her words came out in breathless little puffs.

He nodded, his excitement coming through his hands to hers. "It be crackin' news, Addi. That's what the meeting was about. President Chester Arthur is in town, and he may stop in the pavilion tomorrow for some entertainment after a day of fishing. The president is staying at the Crossmon House as he always does, but they don't have a grand entertainment pavilion as we do. Ain't it dandy news?"

She chuckled. At his brogue or his unveiled excitement, she wasn't sure which. She loved when he bubbled over with enthusiasm, for it always brought out his enchanting Irishness.

"It is. I taught my students about President Arthur and found him an interesting leader. He's a big man— over six feet tall and more than two hundred pounds. But he looks like a president with his clean-shaven chin and those huge sideburns."

Liam let go of one of her hands but held the other as if it were a lifeline. He stroked his chin. "Aye, you don't say? I'd forgotten. Your description will help me spot him when he comes. Tell me more about the man, please. I like to be well-informed when dignitaries visit."

Thankful she had a keen memory for facts, she continued as if she were teaching her class again. "President Arthur is dignified, honest, well liked, and a former teacher, like me. His wife died before he took office, so his sister helped care for his three children and acted as an unofficial first lady."

He leaned in and grinned. "Wasn't he known as the Republican Reformer?"

"He was. He worked hard to reunify the nation after the Civil War." She paused, sad at the next information she had to share. "But I read that he's in poor health of late."

A frown tugged at his lips, and most unfortunately, he let go of her hand. "Sorry to hear that. But tomorrow should prove a special day for us. And hopefully, if we all do our jobs well, for him."

CHAPTER 12

*A*ddi shook off the grouchies—as Papa called it. She had made her choice, and she'd not wallow in the desire to see Gert dealt with properly. Today would be Jimmy's last class with them, so she'd review their time together. She swallowed a pang of sorrow as she wrote on the board, *A good friend is like a four-leaf clover: hard to find and lucky to have.—an Irish saying*

She'd talk about friendship.

Liam had become a good friend, but was he more? His kiss on her hands yesterday made her wonder. And hope. So did the way he looked at her now and then. And the extra attention he'd paid her.

But she'd be leaving soon—to where, she didn't know. He'd be staying here in his fine position as manager of the Thousand Island House hotel pavilion. In the winter, he'd told her one night as they sat under the stars, he worked as a paper-hanger, pasting up the new faddish frieze-filling-dado wallpaper in the homes of the wealthiest families in the county, even taking several jobs for the Watertown elite, including Mr. John Paddock. He had created quite a thriving business. To fall back on, he'd said.

Unwelcome tears threatened to brim over. She'd miss him most of all.

Before long, the children had arrived, and Jimmy had a severe case of the grouchies too. Gone were his ready smile and bright eyes. He sat by himself and didn't speak to anyone. Addi knelt near him and talked with him quietly and compassionately. She knew how he felt.

"Are you sad about leaving, Jimmy? We will miss you terribly, but I'm sure you have friends and family in Buffalo, right?"

He folded his arms and didn't look at her. "Nope, just my old grandmama, and she don't want me no more. Neither does Papa. He won't even take me fishing before we go. He never has time for me."

While she feared that was true, she'd not reveal her feelings. "I'm sure he loves you very much, and so does your grandmama. Your papa's just busy."

"But I wanted to go fishin' and he said no."

Addi rubbed his back. "The Bible says, to everything there is a season. Perhaps this is not the season for you to go fishing. Maybe next summer?"

"It ain't fair." Jimmy glanced at her with teary eyes that turned stormy.

She shook her head and patted his back. "Life isn't fair, but we can still find joy in each and every day. Let's make your last day here special. After circle time, we'll go outside and play hide and seek. Then maybe we'll play Annie Over or Ox in the Ditch."

The boy's eyes lit up. "Ox in the Ditch. It's my favorite."

Addi smiled. "Then Ox in the Ditch it is. In your honor."

After their circle time, in which the children vowed they'd be friends for life, Addi led them off the island to the grassy knoll where they'd flown the kite. Mel was already there with his class but agreed they could all play hide and seek together, and one of the big kids named Norman counted to one hundred before hunting for the children. One by one, he found his classmates and hers, save Jimmy.

Alarm bells clanged in her head, and Addi began shouting—rather unladylike though it be—for Jimmy. Mel took over with his more commanding voice, and the children fanned out, searching for him. Minute after minute, Addi paced and prayed, fidgeted and bit the inside of her cheek until she tasted blood. What if he fell in the river and drowned? Or someone snatched him?

Her heart raced. Her eyes darted back and forth. Slowly, the other children returned. But no Jimmy.

He was lost.

On her watch.

---

*P*resident Chester Arthur sat in the back of the skiff while the boatman steered them toward Wellesley Island. Something under the tarp on the bottom of the boat moved.

What in tarnation?

The boatman snapped his chin toward the island in the distance. "I hear muskie and sturgeon are hanging out on the north side of Wellesley. Wanna catch one, sir?"

Arthur slapped his thigh. "Of course. And pike and bass, if we can. But I want to be back by mid-afternoon to explore the Thousand Island House entertainment pavilion."

The boatman clicked his tongue. "Ain't been in there but hear it has card and table games, billiards, bowling, table tennis, a swimming pool, and a whole heap more. I got to see the hotel when it first opened. Mr. Staples graciously opened it to the local community, just for a day. Oooh-wee! It was the fanciest place I'd ever seen, including in the papers."

Arthur chuckled. A day with this chap might be just what he needed to center him after years in Washington. "All that glitters is not gold, sir. I grew up the son of a poor Baptist preacher in the backwoods of Vermont, and I still prefer small-town simplicity. As an adult, I wore fancy duds and stayed in the most elegant places. When I became a lawyer, I tangled with the custom house bosses and dined with the high and mighty in New York City. But who would ever have guessed this country preacher's son would become vice president and then president after President Garfield was assassinated? I have to say, I've tried the life of lavish style and connections, and I've enjoyed the gilded halls of Washington and fancy hotels like the Thousand Island House, but I'd rather be fishing on the St. Lawrence River with you, my friend. By the way, what's your name?"

The boatman reached up and scratched his head. "Well, I'll be jiggered. Thank ye, sir. My name's Sam."

"Pleased to know you, Sam."

When they reached a small inlet on the eastern shore of Wellesley, Sam dropped anchor. "This'll be a good spot. The fish should still be biting this time of day."

The tarp moved again, so Arthur pointed to it. "What's under that, Sam?"

Sam waved a hand. "Our lunch, some life vests, a bucket. That sort of thing."

"But it moved. Twice."

Sam pulled back the tarp and exposed a small boy curled up in a ball, trembling. "A stowaway? Who are you, child? Speak up or I'll throw you overboard."

The curly-topped boy sat up straight. The child's

dark eyes darted to Arthur's. "Jimmy Worthington, sir. I'm sorry. I just had to go fishin'. I didn't know it'd be with you!" He swallowed as his chin quivered something fierce. "Sir. Mr. President."

President Arthur motioned him close. "Come here, child."

Jimmy scooted toward him on his hands and knees, managing a wobbly bow. "Your majesty."

Arthur held back a chuckle and patted Jimmy's back. "President Arthur is fine. Sit with me, son."

Jimmy obeyed. He sat with his shaking hands pasted together, his shoulders sagging. "Sorry, Mr. Boatman. I should've asked you. But Papa never had time to take me fishing, and we're leaving tomorrow. I had to go fishing. Just once."

President Arthur reached his arm around the boy and drew him close. "I have a son just like you, but he's all grown up now. He would've done the same thing, though he'd be in a heap of trouble when he got home."

"Maybe we should take the tike back?" Sam frowned as he glanced across the channel. "But you'd miss the best time to fish."

Jimmy's eyes trained on Arthur, radiating hope. Truth be told, he reminded him more of himself than his son.

Arthur turned Jimmy to face him. "Your family is probably terribly worried right now, son."

Jimmy shook his head. "Mama is dead and Papa is working. I just hid when we kids were playing hide and seek. They won't miss me none. Not for a while, anyhow."

The president considered it for a moment. He shouldn't stay, but the child wanted to fish even more than he did. And they'd both be leaving in the morning. What to do?

"What if we fish, just for a little while, and then I get you home?"

Sam nodded with a grin.

"I should make you walk the plank, boy. That's what they do with stowaways on the high seas."

Jimmy glanced around the plankless skiff. "Sorry, sir. I'll not do it again. Foolishness made me. It's bound up in my heart."

At that, Arthur guffawed so loudly, Sam had to quiet him down. "You'll scare the fish, sir."

He put a hand to his mouth and lowered his voice. "Sorry. Let's catch some fish, shall we, Jimmy?"

Addi alerted Liam of Jimmy's disappearance, and he called Lieutenant Worthington, who, thankfully, was working on paperwork in his room. All available staff joined in the search, and so did a dozen or more locals. Boatmen scanned the shore for his body. Firemen climbed into the hotel's crawl space. Men inspected every crevasse in the rock outcroppings along the shore. Even townspeople checked the nooks and crannies of their streets for the boy.

No Jimmy.

Addi took her remaining five children back to the classroom and set them to coloring or playing with puzzles. Panic rose by the minute, and her heart ached as though it was breaking. Worry gnawed at her every thought. Her stomach began churning, and sweat broke out on her forehead. She swiped it away and prayed that Jimmy would be found. Soon.

Never had she felt so alone and afraid. Not even when her papa died. This was all her fault. She should've kept the children here, safe and secure, not let them run wild and free with the big kids. If anything happened to the boy, she'd never forgive herself. And neither would Lieutenant Worthington, or Liam, or the townspeople. She'd be a pariah, and her career as a teacher—or anything—would be over. Perhaps she'd even be arrested for murder. She cringed at the thought, and her hands shook. She had successfully bitten back tears for the past two hours, but she could no longer hold them in.

Liam burst through the door and hollered, "He's been found. Come."

She wiped away her tears, her voice catching in her throat. "Safe?"

Liam's grin and an almost imperceptible nod told her the boy was okay. He grabbed hold of her hand. "I want you to hear the story from the rescuer himself."

The children cheered and chased Liam and Addi down to the hotel docks, where Jimmy stood before his father receiving a terrible tongue-lashing in front of everyone. Two fishermen stood by, as did a growing crowd.

Wait! Who was that giant man? She knew that figure. President Arthur? What was he doing there?

President Arthur broke into Lieutenant Worthington's tirade. "I'm sorry to interrupt, sir, but have you never made a mistake? Did you ever want to do something so badly that you disobeyed and did it, anyway? Have mercy on the poor fellow. Please. He's a good boy, and he's back safe and sound. And you can blame me for his late arrival. We enjoyed a little fishing before we returned. He caught his first fish, a feisty sturgeon, but it took a little time to wrestle the thing into our boat. Show him, Sam."

Sam held up a three-foot monster that looked more like a whiskery shark than a fish. The crowd *ooh*ed and *aah*ed and then burst into cheers.

Mercifully, the president's chastisement silenced Lieutenant Worthington, but the lieutenant cast Addi a red-faced glare. "You, Miss Bell, were negligent in your duties. Dismiss her, Donovan. Immediately."

President Arthur glanced at her and clapped the lieutenant on his shoulder. "Now look here, sir. There's no need for a temper or to place blame. The child hid in my boat. We didn't discover him until we were at

Wellesley Island. He is safe. None of that is this poor woman's fault. Let it go, man."

Lieutenant Donovan harrumphed, grabbing Jimmy's hand. "Thank you for keeping my boy safe, sir."

Jimmy shook free of his father and bowed to the president. "Thank you, Mr. President, for the best day of my life!"

President Arthur chuckled and pulled him into a grandfatherly hug. "You take care, James. After catching that sturgeon, you're a man now."

Jimmy—or rather, James—beamed. "I will, sir, and thanks again. You, too, Mr. Sam."

James ran to Addi and hugged her, and the children hugged both. "Sorry I hid in the boat. I didn't know I would get to go fishin' with the president! And I caught a huge fish."

She giggled. "I heard, *James.* You scared us half to death, but I'm just glad you're safe."

"I'm sorry about that. I didn't mean to."

James's bottom lip quivered, and his eyes brimmed with tears. The children patted him and hugged him, pouring grace and mercy and forgiveness upon him. Why couldn't his father do the same?

Addi touched his shoulder. "We all forgive you, James. Maybe your father will let you come back to class for the rest of the day, if you ask him nicely?"

Lieutenant Worthington spoke from behind her, addressing his son instead of Addi. "You may, but no outdoor games, young man."

His tone was softer now—gentle, even. "And I apologize for my temper, miss. This wasn't your doing."

Addi gasped. "Thank you, sir. I'll take good care of him."

The lieutenant smiled. He actually smiled! "I'll count on it."

* * *

Liam enjoyed the entire scene from the sidelines. The outpouring of mercy from the president, from the children, from Addi, warmed his heart. Even Lieutenant Worthington mellowed at long last.

Crisis averted.

The crowd dispersed, and Liam escorted Addi and her class back to the room before preparing for the possibility of the president's visit. After all the hubbub, would he bother with a stop at the pavilion? Liam informed his staff to be ready, and ready they were.

Within minutes, President Arthur came through the door. "Do I need to change, or may I tour the pavilion in my fishing attire?"

Liam smiled. "Welcome, Mr. President. You're most certainly welcome as you are. You'd like a tour?"

Arthur glanced at the many signs directing visitors to the various entertainments. "I would. I come to the islands every year and look forward to enjoying this place. But I'd like to see James's teacher first, please."

Addi? Whatever for? Liam could read no hint on the president's face as to whether his request might bode good or ill for the nursery teacher. "Certainly, sir. This way."

Liam led the president to the classroom and poked his head in the door. "We have a special visitor, children."

The children stopped playing Duck, Duck, Goose. He opened the door wide, and the president stepped into the room.

James jumped up and clapped his hands. "Mr. President!"

President Arthur stepped over to Addi and put out his hand. "I wanted to meet your teacher, James. You had so many good things to say about her."

Addi's cheeks turned a pretty pink, and she blinked rapidly several times, apparently trying to find her tongue. She finally did. "Mr. President. Welcome."

Liam smiled. He hadn't experienced a day like this in...

Well. Ever.

CHAPTER 13

ddi donned her mossy green dress that she had refashioned from her mother's old gown. She took extra time with her hair, tucking it into a tidy chignon, then pinched her cheeks and straightened her shoulders for good measure. Liam had invited her to join him for an evening searchlight tour on the *St. Lawrence* steamer, that beautiful white boat she'd seen so many times.

Today would be a special day, no matter what.

The tempo of her pulse picked up to that of a lively jig. She'd never been asked to do something with a man. She'd never been on a cruise boat that large before, only the small Navy skiff. And a boat tour at night? Her hand trembled as she tried to restrain one rebellious curl and finally gave up. She'd be late for work if she didn't get going. As she left her room and headed toward the pavilion, she sucked in a steadying breath.

So much unknown. Including a searchlight tour on the mighty St. Lawrence River. Moreover, it was her last week at the Thousand Island House, and the beginning of an unchartered future.

As she entered her classroom, pangs of loneliness bombarded her, as they always did when her tomorrows were unclear. She missed Sally and Markie and Jimmy—James—now gone a full two weeks. She smiled at how President Arthur had transformed the tyke into a young man with a fish and a name change. Funny how little things like that could make all the difference in a child's life.

She wanted to touch each of the children's lives as the president had touched Jimmy's, so she needed to focus on her three remaining charges. One week. Just one week left to make her mark—and figure out what she'd do with *her* life. Perhaps find another teaching job? Or move to the big city and become a nanny?

Worry gnawed at her thoughts. With winter coming, she had to find a position and a place to live. Soon.

For now, though, she'd finish well, even if she had just three children to care for. Only Lora, Nora, and Gregory remained, but she'd give them her very best.

Liam came through the door, a scent of shaving cream wafting in and tickling her nose. "Top of the morning to you, lass. Did you hear about Gert? Chef reluctantly fired her after catching her red-handed, stealing from the larder."

She gasped. "No, I was running late, so I came straight here."

Liam shrugged, walking over to the terrarium and tapping on the glass. "Happened late last night. I just heard. Say, what are you going to do with Froggie?"

"I'll set him free *after* the children leave. No sense in causing tears unnecessarily."

He smiled, that handsome crooked smile she'd come to love. Oh, how she'd miss seeing him every day! He brightened her world and filled her heart with longing. A longing she'd never known before. Still, she must guard her heart. He was her supervisor and she a simple nursery worker who would be out of work in a week.

With a sigh, she went to the board to write her daily quote. She felt Liam's eyes on her, so she used her best penmanship and then drew hearts for the dots above the i's. *May the hinges of our friendships never grow rusty. – an Irish saying*

Liam chuckled. "My gran used to say that. I love how you've inspired these wee ones every day you've been here. Your sayings. Your circle time. The way you handle their spats and sputters. You really are a gifted teacher, you know."

Her heart fluttered at his compliment. He'd been tossing accolades her way more and more lately, and it fed her soul better than a king's feast. "Thank you, kind sir."

A twinkle in his eye told her he had more to say. "Speaking of your teaching gift...I heard there was an opening at the local school, so I inquired on your behalf. The position is yours, if you want it."

She blinked, taking in the answer to one of her prayers. Then she let out a high-pitched squeal, like a tiny child, and her words bubbled with joy. "Really? Really and truly? But the school board hasn't even met me."

"Didn't have to. Took my word about you."

She ran to him and patted him on the arm. She would rather have hugged him, but that would have been highly improper. Still... "Oh Liam, thank you so much. I've been fretting about my future, and I feel you just gave me the moon. You've become such a good friend, and I'm glad I'll still be in town. Maybe we can stay friends?"

Liam's eyes grew wide, and he swallowed hard. Did he not want to maintain their friendship? His smile dimmed considerably, but just for a moment. Then he guffawed. "You can count on it, little lass."

Gregory burst through the door, interrupting their banter. "I made this for you, Teacher." He handed her a large, roughly cut-out heart. On it he'd drawn an *I*, a heart, and a *U*. Dozens of tiny hearts danced around the edges of the page.

Addi received her gift, her heart brimming over. "Thank you, Gregory. I'll treasure it always."

"Looks as though I'm not your only admirer." Liam winked, waved, and headed toward the door. "Until tonight, Miss Bell."

The setting sun glowed a dramatic orange as Liam escorted Addi onto the gleaming white *St. Lawrence* steamer, along with several hundred other passengers. He led her to the bow's upper deck railing, facing west. A large flag fluttered in the gentle breeze on its bow, another on a tall mast near the wheelhouse, four smaller flags midship, and an enormous US flag hung on the stern.

In the center of the vessel, a trio played a haunting tune on a harp and two violins which echoed down the hallway and danced on the water, creating a most pleasant beginning to what he hoped would be a magical evening.

Addi leaned on the railing, closed her eyes, and smiled. "Isn't the music wonderful? It sounds like a sunset."

As if she'd forgotten something, her eyes popped open just as the orange ball exploded into reds and yellows and then burst into the prettiest purples and lavenders Liam had ever seen. She gasped and spread her arms as if she were a bird taking flight, almost smacking him in the face. She didn't even notice, so absorbed was she in the moment.

He loved that.

"Oh, Liam, I've never seen such a dramatic, beautiful, wonderful sunset. Can you imagine what heaven must be like if it's this lovely here on earth?"

He studied her face, aflame with the colors of the sunset. "I cannot. But just now, your loveliness comes the closest to an angelic being as I've ever seen."

"Oh Liam, you say the sweetest things." She peeked out of the corners of her eyes, barely turning her head.

"Miss, I only speak the truth." He pasted his hand on his chest as if offended.

The captain stepped out of the wheelhouse and onto the deck. The crowd quieted. In a booming voice, he addressed his passengers. "Ladies and gentlemen. If you think that sunset was lovely, that's just the prelude. Our one-million candlepower searchlight with its forty-eight-inch parabolic mirror will take us on a unique and magical tour of the islands. In the dark, starry night, you'll see the Thousand Islands as you've never seen them before. We'll navigate through narrow channels and around islands. We may even see a muskie happily popping its head out of the water to bid you good evening. Now, enjoy the refreshments, the music, and the magic of our Thousand Islands Searchlight Tour."

The crowd clapped and cheered, and the familiar whistle, whose distinctive chime note could be heard whenever the steamer left the dock, sounded loud and clear.

Liam chuckled. "You'll hear those hisses of steam from the whistle throughout the evening. One blast signals something is dead ahead, two is for starboard, and three is for port. They sound it when they spot buoys and other official markers, private markers, or something else that might prove a danger. Navigating the river in the day is tricky enough. Night navigation must be done with the utmost care."

"Is it safe?" Addi's eyes flashed with sudden fear.

He took her hand in his. "I wouldn't bring you if it wasn't. Fear not. This crew has been navigating these waters, day and night, for years."

As the sky darkened and it became hard to see beyond the boat, Liam intertwined his fingers with Addi's.

She glanced down at their hands, and a hint of a smile dangled on her lips. But then her hand gave a tiny tremor before she squeezed it. "What is this, Liam?"

I love you, that's what!

Wait, lad. Not yet. Like a sailboat in a dead calm, his breath caught in his throat and lodged there. His mind went blank. For several moments, he frantically searched his foggy brain for something to say as she searched his face for an answer.

"Have you not noticed that I care for you, Addison Bell? I love how you embrace every moment with the whimsical wonder of a child, yet you're altogether a lovely and accomplished woman and teacher. And I adore that you have a deep-seated desire to overcome the most arduous task with a pretty smile and unceasing energy. It says a lot about your character. About you."

Addi tilted her head and furrowed her brow as if he spoke German. "Um...thank you?"

Suddenly, the spotlight shone on the starboard side. They were in a narrow channel where huge rocks could be seen on both sides.

An older woman harrumphed. "They don't need to show off for us. We'd be safer out in the main channel where we belong."

Liam let go of her hand and pointed to the shore. "See there, four large bucks. Aye, look at those antlers, will ya?"

Addi leaned over the railing. Even in the dark, her face fairly shone with joy. "Oh, they're beautiful."

The spotlight turned off and they were in the dark again. The violins and harp played a waltz, and couples began to dance.

"May I have this dance?" Liam took her hand.

She curtsied and allowed him to take her in his arms. Her glistening eyes rivaled the starry sky above them. What was she thinking?

As he led her in a waltz, curiosity got the better of him. "Penny for your thoughts, my sweet?"

Her mouth made a perfect *O* before she answered. "The thought of this beautiful summer coming to an end makes me sad. Though, thanks to you, I have a teaching position, I only have a week left before I'm homeless and alone again."

The signal sounded once, and the searchlight turned on again, drawing their attention in the direction of the light. Several large fish shone just below the surface of the water, and night birds skittered in its light. The crowd *ooh*ed and *ahh*ed. But as Liam strained to see the true reason for the sounding, straight ahead, a rowboat with a clueless couple in it drifted dangerously into their path. The steamer sounded again, alerting the young lovers of their perilous course. When the man realized what was happening, he took to rowing furiously until they disappeared into the darkness.

Addi's hands flew to her mouth, and she prayed. "Good Lord, protect that couple. Please."

"Another reason I adore you." Liam put his arm around her.

"Don't play with my heart, Liam. I cannot bear it." Her hands dropped to her sides, and a frown tipped tears out of her eyes until they rolled down her cheeks.

Liam grabbed her hand and tugged her to a quiet corner. He took both hands in his and kissed them as he'd done before. "Have you not heard the Scripture that says, *out of the abundance of the heart the mouth speaks*? That's why I say the things I do. My heart is full of you. Full of...love for you."

"Oh!"

Like a dam had burst, he found his tongue. "I love you, Addison Bell. I want to experience your child-like wonder, your unfailing wisdom, and your womanly ways for the rest of my life. You give my life joy and meaning. Aye, you've become my North Star. Will you do me the honor of being my wife? Please?"

Addi's cute little brow furrowed as it so often did, but her eyes didn't seem to register what he was asking. Would she say no?

The excruciating moments ticked on as though time was grinding to a halt. She licked her lips, and ever so slowly, a small smile twitched her cheeks. Like a warm sunrise, it grew, rising to her eyes and melting them like liquid chocolate. Quivering fingers pulled his hands to her lips, and she kissed them. Twice.

"Does that mean yes?" An exasperated chuckle escaped his lips.

She threw back her head and giggled, dropped his hands, and flung her arms around his neck. "Yes! Yes! Yes!"

"Well, I'll be jiggered. I do believe I'm the luckiest lad on this earth!" Liam kissed her on the cheek before prying her arms from him. He wanted to see her face. To kiss it.

Several people nearby broke out into cheers, thwarting his plan to kiss her properly. News spread quickly. Like wildfire. Strangers congratulated them, stealing their special moment, never to be found again.

Blathers! That wasn't how he'd planned for it to go at all.

The spotlight shone again, illuminating a lighthouse. "That's Sunken Rock Lighthouse, my bride-to-be." The words rolled off his tongue like honey. *She said yes!* His pulse danced a jig, and he felt as if he could soar like an eagle.

A sailor materialized beside them. "Captain wants to see you, sir. Her too. Please follow me."

Addi's face displayed the same confusion he felt, but they obeyed the sailor, following him up to the wheelhouse. The spotlight shut off again, leaving them with only stars and moon as their light.

The captain turned the steamer over to his first mate and stepped out of the tiny room. "I hear congratulations are in order."

Addi curtsied and Liam nodded. "Yes, sir."

The white-haired captain grinned. "Any reason that you shouldn't get married right here and now? As captain, I have the credentials to do so, and I'd love to celebrate your nuptials on this very night."

Dumbstruck for the second time that night, Liam looked at Addi, who gazed at the stars. Did she even hear the captain's offer?

"Addi, did you hear him? Is that a fool idea?"

Neither had family—or many friends, for that matter—to celebrate with them. They'd be starting their own. Right now?

Addi whispered in his ear. "Let's. Under God's

perfect canopy of stars. On this magical, marvelous night."

Liam took her hand, kissed it, and nodded to the captain. "Let's do it!"

The End

Did you enjoy this book? We hope so!
**Would you take a quick minute to leave a review
where you purchased the book?**
It doesn't have to be long. Just a sentence or two telling
what you liked about the story!

Receive a FREE ebook and get updates when new Wild
Heart books release: https://wildheartbooks.org/
newsletter

ABOUT THE AUTHOR

Susan G Mathis is an international award-winning, multi-published author of stories set in the beautiful Thousand Islands, her childhood stomping ground in upstate NY. Susan has been published more than twenty-five times in full-length novels, novellas, and non-fiction books. She has seven in her fiction line including, *The Fabric of Hope: An Irish Family Legacy, Christmas Charity, Katelyn's Choice, Devyn's Dilemma,*

Sara's Surprise, Reagan's Reward, and *Colleen's Confession, Peyton's Promise,* and *Rachel's Reunion. Mary's Moment* came out in May, 2023. Susan's book awards include three Illumination Book Awards, three American Fiction Awards, two Indie Excellence Book Awards, and two Literary Titan Book Awards. *Reagan's Reward* is a Selah Awards finalist.

Before Susan jumped into the fiction world, she served as the Founding Editor of *Thriving Family* magazine and the former Editor/Editorial Director of twelve Focus on the Family publications. Her first two published books were nonfiction. *Countdown for Couples: Preparing for the Adventure of Marriage* with an Indonesian and Spanish version, and *The ReMarriage Adventure: Preparing for a Life of Love and Happiness*, have helped thousands of couples prepare for marriage. Susan is also the author of two picture books, *Lexie's Adventure in Kenya* and *Princess Madison's Rainbow Adventure.* Moreover, she is published in various book compilations including five *Chicken Soup for the Soul* books, *Ready to Wed, Supporting Families Through Meaningful Ministry, The Christian Leadership Experience,* and *Spiritual Mentoring of Teens.* Susan has also several hundred magazine and newsletter articles.

Susan is president of American Christian Fiction Writers-CS (ACFW), former vice president of Christian Authors Network (CAN), and a member of Christian

Independent Publishing Association (CIPA). For over twenty years, Susan has been a speaker at writers' conferences, teachers' conventions, writing groups, and other organizational gatherings. Susan makes her home in Colorado Springs and enjoys traveling around the world but returns each summer to the islands she loves. Visit www.SusanGMathis.com for more.

ACKNOWLEDGMENTS

I hope you enjoy *A Summer at Thousand Island House*. If you've read any of my other books, you know that I love introducing history to my readers through fictional stories. I hope this story sparks interest in our amazing past, especially the fascinating past of the marvelous Thousand Islands. The Thousand Island House is real, and so are the amazing visitors to the resort, but please note that I took a bit of creative license in bringing this story to life, as some of the timing is a little different than recorded.

Thanks to you, my readers, for your faithful support and for staying connected. I love hearing from you. And special thanks ...

To Judy Keeler, my wonderful historical editor, who combs through my manuscripts for accuracy. Because of her, you can trust that my stories are historically correct.

To my wonderful editor, Denise Weimer, for being a great friend and for sharing your talents with me.

To my amazing beta readers Laurie, Barb, Donna, Melinda, and Davalynn, for all your hard work and wise input.

To my many writer friends who so willingly write endorsements and reviews, encourage me in my writing, and pray for me. There are too many to name here, but you know who you are. Thank you.

And to all my dear friends who have journeyed with me in my writing. Thanks for your emails, social media posts, and especially for your reviews. Most of all, thanks for your friendship.

And to God, from whom all good gifts come. Without You, there would never be a dream or the ability to fulfill that dream. Thank you!

Please stay in touch at susangmathis@gmail.com

If you love historical romance, check out the other Wild Heart books!

Marisol ~ Spanish Rose by Elva Cobb Martin

Escaping to the New World is her only option...Rescuing her will wrap the chains of the Inquisition around his neck.

Marisol Valentin flees Spain after murdering the nobleman who molested her. She ends up for sale on the indentured servants' block at Charles Town harbor —dirty, angry, and with child. Her hopes are shattered, but she must find a refuge for herself and the child she carries. Can this new land offer her the grace, love, and security she craves? Or must she escape again to her only living relative in Cartagena?

Captain Ethan Becket, once a Charles Town minister, now sails the seas as a privateer, grieving his deceased wife. But when he takes captive a ship full of indentured servants, he's intrigued by the woman whose manners seem much more refined than the average Spanish serving girl. Perfect to become governess for his young son. But when he sets out on a quest to find his captured sister, said to be in Cartagena, little does he expect his new Spanish governess to stow away on his ship with her six-month-old son. Yet her offer of help to free his sister is too tempting to pass up. And her beauty, both inside and out, is too attractive for his heart to protect itself against—until he learns she is a wanted murderess.

As their paths intertwine on a journey filled with danger, intrigue, and romance, only love and the grace of God can overcome the past and ignite a new beginning for Marisol and Ethan.

Rocky Mountain Redemption by Lisa J. Flickinger

A Rocky Mountain logging camp may be just the place to find herself.

To escape the devastation caused by the breaking of her wedding engagement, Isabelle Franklin joins her aunt in the Rocky Mountains to feed a camp of lumberjacks cutting on the slopes of Cougar Ridge. If only she could out run the lingering nightmares.

Charles Bailey, camp foreman and Stony Creek's itinerant pastor, develops a reputation to match his new nickname — Preach. However, an inner battle ensues when the details of his rough history threaten to over-come the beliefs of his young faith.

Amid the hazards of camp life, the unlikely friendship growing between the two surprises Isabelle. She's drawn to Preach's brute strength and gentle nature as he leads the ragtag crew toiling for Pollitt's Lumber. But when the ghosts from her past return to haunt her, the choices she will make change the course of her life forever—and that of the man she's come to love.

Lone Star Ranger by Renae Brumbaugh Green

Elizabeth Covington will get her man.

And she has just a week to prove her brother isn't the murderer Texas Ranger Rett Smith accuses him of being. She'll show the good-looking lawman he's wrong, even if it means setting out on a risky race across Texas to catch the real killer.

Rett doesn't want to convict an innocent man. But he can't let the Boston beauty sway his senses to set a guilty man free. When Elizabeth follows him on a dangerous trek, the Ranger vows to keep her safe. But who will protect him from the woman whose conviction and courage leave him doubting everything—even his heart?

Don't miss the next book in Romance at the Gilded Age
Resorts Series!